AFRICAN SAFARI ADVENTURES

Volume 1

THE ANT-LION

Tony Irvin

Tony Irvin

Equator **EP** Press

Second edition
Equator Press, an imprint of Write Now! Publications.
www: writenowgroup.co.uk

Copyright © 2018 Tony Irvin

First edition published by Matador, 2009,
Kindle edition, 2011 as:
The Ant-Lion

Design and typesetting: george@wickerswork.co.uk

Kindle ISBN: 978-1-912955-00-8
Paperback ISBN: 978-1-912955-01-5

SOME AMAZON REVIEWS FROM THE FIRST EDITION

This book is the BEST book I have ever read. The best part of it was that it was really informative, like it tells you what 'hello' is in Swahili. I really enjoyed this book because... I was able to imagine what the characters, the land and the animals looked like.

This was an excellent book. It made you just want to read on and on. The adventures were extraordinary and very exciting. The setting suited the story very very well. It told me many facts about the Maasai people.

I read this book and thought it was utterly fabulous! It was really interesting and fun. The adventure was great, I wish I could have been there!

The Ant-Lion was fantastic! It ticked all the right boxes. It was funny and the description was ace. The Ant-Lion had a really good story line to it and it flowed really well.

I'm reading this book to my 9-year-old son every night and he loves it. The chapters are a perfect length to read aloud... My son's school has a link with Tanzania and has had visitors from the country and this book has really captured his imagination.

My 7-year-old son was given this as a present and I read it to him at bedtime- we were both so engrossed that his light went off much later than it should have done.

The Ant-Lion is an outstanding book! It is exciting and a must read. I really enjoyed this book and couldn't wait to pick it up each day to find out what was going to happen next.

Do not read unless you are prepared for complete inability to put it down!

Warning to Readers

Don't read this book if you're afraid of elephants.

Chapter 1

The Letter

Lucy glared at the cartoon rat on the cereal packet which was urging her to take up swimming.

'Get a life,' she muttered, and scowled round the breakfast table on a grey rainy morning. 'Huh. Welcome to England in February.'

The kitchen door flew open and slammed against the radiator. Kal, her eleven-year-old brother, burst in, his shirt hanging out, his tie twisted and his hair sticking up like a startled hedgehog.

Caspar, Lucy's cat, let out a yowl and dived under the table.

'Oh, for goodness sake!' yelled Lucy. She scrabbled under the table to rescue Caspar and nicked some bacon from Dad's plate to calm him.

'Kal, do try not to charge around like that,' said Mum. 'Tuck your shirt in and—'

'But someone's written to us from Tasmania,' he cried, waving a letter.

Ellie, who was cooking Kal's breakfast, snatched the letter. 'Tanzania, you wally. Not Tasmania.'

'Ah,' said Dad, looking up from the magazine he was reading. 'That'll be for me. I've been invited to—'

'The letter's addressed to Mum,' said Ellie.

Lucy perked up. 'Who do we know in Tanzania?'

'Reuben Kalima?' suggested Kal.

'Who?'

'Reuben Kalima, the Olympic medallist?'

'You know an Olympic medallist?'

'Well, I sort of know him.'

'Just because you can run,' said Ellie, 'and have been nicknamed after him, hardly means you—'

'My breakfast!'

1

'Sorree!' Ellie dropped the letter, thrust the smoking pan into the sink and turned on the cold tap. There was a great hiss and the kitchen filled with steam.

'You're not supposed to do that,' said Lucy.

'So?' Ellie turned off the tap and flapped at the steam.

'Really, Ellie, you're twelve now, you should know better,' said Mum.

'I *said* I was sorry.'

Mum retrieved the letter from the floor, turned off the cooker and switched on the extractor fan.

Kal peered into the sink. 'Yuk! I'm not eating that.'

'Cook your own next time.' Ellie plonked herself down at the table and began texting her friends.

'It's all right, Kal. I'll cook you some more,' said Mum.

'Who's the letter from?' asked Lucy.

'Good gracious, it's my cousin Craig,' said Mum. 'What a lovely surprise. We haven't been in touch for ages. I wonder why he's…' She began reading.

'What is it, Mum?' asked Lucy.

'Probably something bad,' muttered Kal.

'No. Listen to this: *Dear Sarah, Please excuse my writing to you out of the blue, but I wonder if I could ask a big favour of David—*'

'Me?' said Dad.

'Just listen! *I now manage a wildlife ranch in Tanzania—*'

'Wow,' breathed Lucy, who even at ten, had decided to become a wildlife vet. 'A real wildlife ranch.'

'Shh. *—and am developing a programme of conservation which integrates the needs of the wildlife with those of the local Maasai people and their livestock.*'

'What's integrate?' asked Lucy.

'Stop interrupting,' said Ellie.

'It means both the needs of wildlife and local people will be considered together,' said Mum. 'Listen to this, though: *However, we're finding it increasingly difficult to meet the rising costs of running the ranch and need to explore ways to increase our income. I've heard there is an international geology conference in Arusha in July and wonder if David will be attending. If so, could he spare some time to visit* the ranch because we believe there may be deposits of valuable minerals in—'

'What sort of minerals?' asked Dad.

'He doesn't say.'

'Probably diamonds,' said Lucy. 'They're found in Africa.'

Ellie snorted.

'Are you going, Dad?' asked Kal.

'I certainly plan to.'

'Will you be able to help Craig?' asked Mum.

'I'll have to see. The conference is the priority but I could probably find some time to...' Dad's voice trailed off. 'What's the matter with that cat?'

'He's puking,' said Kal.

'Gross,' said Ellie, still texting. 'Put him outside.'

'Not my cat. You do it.'

'Kal, what's your problem?'

'I don't do animals.'

Lucy jumped up, grabbed the heaving cat and just managed to get him outside before he threw up several large pieces of bacon. 'Oops,' she said. Then leaving Caspar to sort himself out went back inside. 'Fur ball,' she announced, but no one took any notice.

'...an important international conference,' Dad was saying, 'I've been invited to give the opening talk on the first day – great honour.'

'Can we come?' asked Lucy.

'Certainly not.'

'Why? You're always saying we need to broaden our horizons – whatever that's supposed to mean.'

Dad scowled. 'Well, er, I'll be... I'll be extremely busy. And you couldn't possibly stay in the hotel – far too expensive.'

'Craig says we'd be welcome to stay at Simba Ranch,' said Mum, scanning the letter again.

'That's settled then,' said Lucy.

Dad held up his hand. 'Wait. We need to discuss this.'

'We already have.'

'We can't rush into things,' said Dad. 'There are all sorts of

3

considerations to take into account.'

'Like what?'

'Like… like your schooling.'

'We break up in July,' said Ellie.

'Well… well, the cat then,' cried Dad triumphantly. 'We can't take him.'

'Who'd want to take that old rat-bag?' muttered Kal.

'He's not a rat-bag!' yelled Lucy.

'It's all right, darling,' said Mum. 'I'm sure Caspar can stay with Mrs Knight next door. He'll be very happy there.'

'All fixed, then,' said Lucy.

'Just a minute.' Dad held up his hand. 'What about—?'

'And I could take leave from work,' added Mum.

'There, all sorted.' Lucy gave Dad a beaming smile. 'That wasn't difficult, was it?'

Six weeks later, he came home with the tickets.

Chapter 2

Rat-Man

'Fupi, I've arrived. I'm here – actually here in Tanzania,' whispered Lucy, stroking the little dog sitting on her lap.

Fupi, Craig's terrier who had immediately attached herself to Lucy, wagged her tail.

'I can't wait to get to Simba.'

Simba: the wildlife ranch managed by Mum's cousin, Craig, had previously been just a name, a dot on a map of Africa. Lucy could hardly believe she would be there later today. This was going to be the best holiday ever.

Craig had met the family at the airport where the temperature was a hundred degrees hotter than when they'd left London. Now they were outside a hotel in the town of Arusha, sipping drinks in the shade of a tree full of chattering yellow birds building nests that looked like grass tennis balls. Lucy fumbled in her rucksack for her new bird book and noticed Craig smiling.

'What?'

'They're masked weavers,' he said. 'Here.' He showed her the place in the book.

'Brilliant! My first African bird. I'm going to make a list of all the different ones I see.'

'Good for you, Lucy. I'll help.'

'Big deal,' muttered Kal, who was playing some sort of game on his phone – as usual.

Ellie was reading a book and twiddling a strand of hair – as usual. And Mum was rabbiting on – as usual; this time about how exciting it was coming to East Africa for the first time.

Dad had gone into the hotel to register for the conference on rocks he was attending. Rocks! How boring was that – even if you were a geologist?

'This is such a brilliant place, Fupi,' whispered Lucy. She

5

gave a contented sigh and looked around. The sunlit pavements were packed with people jostling for space. Most didn't seem to be doing very much, but Lucy supposed some were shopping while those in smart clothes probably worked in offices. Several sat on the pavement trying to sell bananas, beadwork and stuff. Others were begging. Groups of women, with babies strapped on their backs and baskets on their heads, blocked the pavements as they gossiped with each other.

Vehicles with revving engines and smoking exhausts filled the road. Bicycles zigzagged between them. Dogs – and even goats – wandered wherever they chose. Handcarts, carrying fruit, clothes and bits of cars, were being pulled by sweaty men trying to squeeze through the traffic. One cart even carried a moaning cow, its legs tied together with rope.

Bicycle bells, car horns, reggae music and stall-holders shouting, all added to the racket.

Kal caught Lucy's eye and shook his head. 'This is just so random.'

A scruffy man in rags came shuffling by and held out his hand. Lucy and Kal shrank back. Fupi growled. The man spat on the pavement and moved on.

'Gross,' muttered Kal.

A foghorn blared.

Lucy and Kal spun round to see a silver-grey vehicle forcing its way through the traffic. When it reached the hotel, the driver – an important-looking man in a suit – parked in a no-waiting area and went inside.

Lucy nudged Kal. 'That man looked just like a toad.'

Kal sniggered. 'Cool vehicle, though. First time I've seen a V8 supercharged Vogue SE Range Rover.'

'Looks like a car to me,' said Lucy. She grabbed his arm. 'Kal, those two men!'

'What men?'

'There, on the other side of the street.'

'What about them?'

'They look really creepy.'

One of the men was thickset and had some sort of red

6

blanket over his shoulder. The other, who was taller, glanced around, crossed the busy street and sauntered past the Range Rover, peering in the windows as he did so. He wore a black T-shirt with the word "Death" written beneath a rat dripping blood from vampire-like teeth.

'That T-shirt's wicked,' said Kal. 'Wish I had one like that.'

Rat-Man nodded to the other man who came and joined him.

'Kal, we should say something,' whispered Lucy.

'Like what?'

Rat-Man walked slowly round the vehicle then leaned against the driver's door and began picking his teeth. Both men glanced towards the hotel entrance, and before Lucy had a chance to think, Rat-Man opened the door and slipped into the driving seat.

'Hey!' Lucy tried to catch Craig's attention.

'I'm talking to Craig,' said Mum. 'Don't interrupt!'

The man started the engine.

'But there's two—'

'Two what?'

The important-looking man came hurrying onto the terrace. Lucy made frantic signals and pointed at the Range Rover, but the man merely glared, opened the passenger's door, threw in his briefcase and climbed into the seat beside Rat-Man.

Lucy's voice trailed off. 'Nothing.'

'Really, Lucy,' said Mum. 'You *must* learn not to interrupt like that.'

The thickset man jumped into the back, and the vehicle shot out in front of a bus.

The bus driver honked and had to slam on his brakes.

The Range Rover sped off with Rat-Man shaking his fist out of the window.

Lucy was left gaping after them. Surely, men in smart suits – even if they did look like toads – shouldn't let themselves be driven off in expensive vehicles by such dodgy-looking characters.

Chapter 3

The Briefcase

'Who's that?' asked Mum, indicating a tall man in dark glasses who'd come onto the hotel terrace and seemed to be looking in their direction.

Craig turned in his seat and his face lit up. 'He's a policeman.' He waved to the man to come and join them.

'Perhaps he's come about the car,' said Lucy.

'Car? What car?'

'I just thought he might sort of… like…' Lucy buried her face in Fupi's neck to hide her confusion. She was rescued by the arrival of the policeman at their table.

'Hey, man, good to see you,' said Craig. 'Grab a seat.' He pulled out a chair and signalled to a waiter.

'So what brings you to Arusha?' the policeman asked.

'I've been collecting these good people from the airport.'

Mum scrambled to her feet. 'I'm Sarah Bartlett, Craig's cousin,' she said, holding out her hand and giving a twittery sort of breathless laugh. 'He's invited us all to stay on Simba Ranch. Isn't that lovely? This is Ellie and her sister Lucy. And this is Alan but we call him Kal, after Reuben Kalima the famous runner from your country.' She came up for air.

'Is that so?' said the policeman, shaking Mum's hand.

Lucy squirmed in her seat. This was *so* embarrassing.

'Yes, Kal's a very good runner. He's got the right build, you see. Rather like yours, I suppose.' Another gulp of air. 'I'm sorry; I didn't catch your name.'

The man smiled. 'My name is Reuben Kalima. Welcome to Tanzania.'

'Oh!' Mum sat down suddenly. 'I thought Craig said you were a policeman.'

'I am a policeman.'

Kal's mouth dropped open. 'Are you Reuben Kalima who

8

won the Olympic steeplechase?'

Reuben removed his dark glasses.

'You *are*.'

'Don't stare,' hissed Ellie.

Kal snapped his mouth shut but his eyes remained wide open.

'I wish I could join you on Simba,' said Reuben, sitting down next to Mum. 'It's a great place.'

'Does *simba* mean lion king?' asked Lucy.

'No, thicko, *simba* means lion,' said Ellie.

'We took the children to see this wonderful musical,' explained Mum.

Reuben smiled politely.

'Are there any lions on the ranch, Craig?' asked Lucy.

'Plenty, but that's not how it got its name. The house is built near a hill which the local people think looks like a resting lion. They call it, *Mlima ya Simba*.'

'The Hill of the Lion,' murmured Ellie.

'*Unasema kiswahili?*' cried Craig. 'You speak Swahili?'

Ellie blushed. 'I, er... I'm trying to learn,' she said, holding up her book: *Swahili in Six Weeks*.

Fat chance, thought Lucy.

'Hey, man, that's great.'

'Ellie's very good at languages,' said Mum.

'Mu-u-um!'

'But you are.'

'It's because she eats lots of fish,' explained Lucy, 'but it doesn't work for me.'

Craig and Reuben laughed.

'Do the lions come near the house?' asked Kal.

'Depends what you mean,' said Craig. 'We haven't actually had them inside, but I once found one sleeping on the veranda. He got quite a fright when I tripped over him in the dark. So did I!'

'Oh dear. I do hope it's safe.' Mum took a quick sip of her drink.

Reuben turned to Craig. 'Lucky I saw you as I was passing. I

9

wanted to ask if that trouble you told me about has been sorted yet?'

Craig shook his head. 'I wish I could find out who's behind it.'

'Trouble?' said Mum. 'What are we talking about?'

'Oh, some local nonsense,' said Craig, waving a dismissive hand. 'Nothing you need worry about.'

'You'll let me know, though, Craig, if you need any help,' said Reuben.

'Sure.'

Reuben finished his drink and rose to his feet. 'Thanks for the drink, Craig. I'm afraid I have to leave.' He smiled round the group. 'Enjoy your stay on Simba.'

'Do you think I could have your autograph?' asked Kal.

'Of course.'

Kal scrabbled in his bag. 'I'm afraid that's all I've got,' he said, passing over his boarding pass.

Reuben took a pen from his pocket and wrote: "*From one Kal to another. Welcome to Tanzania, Reuben Kalima.*" He then shook hands with everyone and left.

Kal gazed at his boarding pass in disbelief. 'That is epic.'

Dad came hurrying out of the hotel. 'I seem to have lost my briefcase.'

'Oh, no!' cried Mum.

'It's not here,' said Lucy, peering under the table.

'But, David, I thought you had it with you,' said Mum.

'I did. I had it when I was at the reception desk registering for the conference.'

'Was there anything valuable in it?' asked Craig.

'Dad, our passports,' cried Ellie.

'It's all right, I've got those,' said Mum.

'Geology papers,' said Dad. 'Then there was my talk for the conference, but I can always print another copy. Also those maps you sent me, Craig, showing the possible mineral sites on the ranch.'

'The maps aren't valuable,' said Craig. 'I can always get more.'

'I know, but I'd pencilled some notes on them. It would be tiresome having to repeat the work.'

'Dad, you know you're always forgetting where you put things,' said Ellie.

'Not important things. This is most annoying.'

'You mustn't worry,' said Mum. 'I'm sure the briefcase will turn up.'

'I suppose so.' Dad frowned. 'Perhaps I put it down when that man distracted me.'

'What man?' said Lucy.

'A man who came up and started asking me about Simba Ranch.'

'Someone you knew?' said Mum.

'No. It was strange; he seemed to know me, and he knew you, Craig.'

'What did he look like?'

'An African, quite thick-set and wearing a suit.'

'Did he look like a toad?' asked Lucy.

'A toad!'

'Yes. Did he have sticky-out eyes and a mouth like a letter-box?'

'What are you—?'

'David, how you doin', buddy?' A man with baggy shorts and sunburned knees clapped Dad on the back.

'Vernon. I was hoping you'd be coming to the conference. I want to ask you about your recent paper on pyroclastic flows,' said Dad, all thoughts of the missing briefcase forgotten.

'We're going to stay on a wildlife ranch,' said Lucy.

'Well you enjoy it, little lady.'

'I'm going to be a wildlife vet when I—'

'This is my family,' said Dad, frowning at Lucy.

'Hi, folks, you havin' a good time?'

'Yes, thank you,' chorused the children.

'Professor Vernon, er, um, is an American colleague of mine,' said Dad, taking his friend's arm and leading him away. 'Vernon, there are a couple of points I'd like to clarify with you about your hypothesis on...' He turned to the family. 'Excuse

11

me, I have to…'

'Bye, Dad,' murmured Ellie. 'Nice meeting you.'

'Bye, Professor Er Um,' said Kal.

'These geologists and their rocks,' said Mum, shaking her head. 'It's all they can think about once they get together.'

Craig smiled. 'We hope, though, that David can put his knowledge to good use when he comes to Simba after the conference.'

'What will happen if Dad doesn't find diamonds or whatever?' asked Ellie.

'We keep cattle as well,' said Craig, 'so we might struggle on as a cattle ranch. If not, we'd have to close down. We couldn't pay the staff, couldn't maintain the roads, poachers would come and kill the animals, the Maasai people who share the ranch with us might have to move away – that sort of thing.'

'That sounds awful,' said Lucy.

'Yes, Lucy, it does.' He got to his feet. 'But let's not spoil your holiday. Come on, time to go. But first, I just want to check something. Back in a moment.'

Mum turned to the children. 'Now are you sure you'll be all right while your father and I stay for the conference?'

'We'll be fine,' said Kal.

'I do hope so. Have you remembered your toothbrushes?'

'Mu-u-um.'

'Oh well… Now, do exactly as Craig tells you.' Mum hugged each of them in turn. 'And don't forget to put on plenty of sun cream. The sun can be very—'

'You guys all set?' asked Craig, returning from inside the hotel.

'Bye, Mum,' called the children, and followed Craig onto the pavement.

'Is something wrong?' asked Lucy, noticing his worried expression.

'It's probably nothing.'

'What's probably nothing?'

He stopped and turned to her. 'Your dad's briefcase wasn't at reception.'

Chapter 4

Simba Ranch

Craig led the way along the crowded pavement. Lucy was beside him trying to hold back Fupi who was straining on her a lead, desperate to get back to Simba. Kal and Ellie followed close behind.

'I hope it's not much further,' said Ellie, pushing damp hair out of her face. 'I'm boiling.'

'Soon be there,' said Craig.

'Where are we going?' asked Lucy, trying to make herself heard above Arusha's noisy and smelly traffic.

'To get a taxi.'

'We're going to Simba by taxi?'

Craig glanced over his shoulder. 'No. In my plane.'

'Your plane!' said Kal. 'You've got your own plane?'

'Sure – best way to get around out there. Do you fly?'

Kal hesitated. 'Well, I er, can sort of like fly a Tornado.'

'What rubbish,' said Ellie, struggling to keep up. 'You can operate a Play Station from the sofa.'

'It's more than you can do,' said Kal. 'You crash every time.'

'I guess I'd be the same,' said Craig, turning to cross the road. 'I reckon flying a Cessna is a bit easier than a—'

'Look out!' yelled Lucy.

A clapped-out car came snarling through the traffic.

Ellie screamed.

Craig, who was halfway across the road, just managed to leap aside and roll clear.

'Are you all right?' cried Kal.

'I'm fine,' said Craig, scrambling to his feet. 'That's what happens when you're busy talking.'

'Looked like the driver did that on purpose,' said Lucy.

Craig brushed the dust off his clothes. 'No. It was my fault. I wasn't paying attention.'

'I reckon that was Rat-Man driving,' said Kal.

'Rat-Man?' said Craig. 'Who's that?'

'He was at the hotel. I recognised the T-shirt. Lucy tried to tell you.'

'Kal, you do talk nonsense sometimes,' said Ellie. 'Toad-Face, Rat-Man; it's all those horror books you read.'

'What about Dad's briefcase, then?'

'What about it?'

'I bet it was Toad-Face who nicked it. I saw him with a briefcase when he got into the Range Rover.'

Ellie rolled her eyes. 'Don't you mean his spaceship?'

Kal glared at her. 'You wait and see.'

'Come on, guys,' said Craig. 'Taxis are just round this corner.'

***

The taxi turned off the main road, through a gateway and stopped in front of a single-storey building.

'I thought we were going to the airport,' said Lucy.

'This is it,' said Craig. 'I know it's not quite Kilimanjaro International Airport but it's fine for small planes. Out you get.'

Craig paid the driver while the children collected their rucksacks. They then followed him through the building to where small single-engine planes were parked in neat rows.

'Here we are.' Craig stopped beside one of the planes and Fupi wagged her tail.

'Cool,' said Kal.

'It looks ever so small,' said Ellie.

'You sound like Mum,' said Kal.

'No, I don't!'

Craig slid the front seats forward to make room for them. 'Climb aboard. Ellie and Lucy first,' he said, lifting up Fupi.

The girls struggled into the awkward space with its two seats, clipped on their belts and looked nervous.

Craig winked at them. 'You guys'll be fine,' he said, passing Fupi to Lucy.

'Can she sit on my lap?'

'Sure.'

Craig slid the front seat back into position. 'Right, Kal, you

sit there.' He then climbed in beside h_
headphones and shut the door. 'We'll run
and checks.' He indicated the two sets of c
them. 'Probably not as complicated as a T_
with a grin.

Kal tried to grin back.

'This switch operates the internal light,' said C
one the landing lights, fuel primer here, master elec
spare set of ignition keys tucked under the visor her_

Lucy and Ellie exchanged anxious glances.

When Craig started the engine the noise was deaf_
turned in his seat. 'You guys ready?' he shouted. 'S_
secure?'

The girls nodded and Lucy clung tight to Fupi.

Craig spoke to the control tower, revved up the engine
taxied onto the runway. And that was it. In no time, they w_
off the ground and flying over the Arusha National Park. Cr_
banked the plane round as they climbed higher.

'Ngurdoto Crater,' he shouted, pointing to the extinct
volcano beneath them. Its slopes were covered in thick forest,
and the crater – once a cauldron of molten rock – was now a
green oasis. In the middle were what appeared to be greyish
mice.

'Elephants,' mouthed Craig, above the noise of the plane.

Lucy couldn't believe it. She then saw some ants which were
apparently buffaloes. Things they had previously seen only on
television were there – right below them.

Craig pointed out to the right. 'Mount Kilimanjaro,' he
shouted. 'Highest mountain in Africa.'

'What's the white on the top?' Lucy shouted back.

'Snow.'

'But we're almost on the equator.'

'It's around six thousand metres – cold enough for
permanent snow.'

'Wow!'

'Lot less now than there used to be, thanks to global
warming.' He pointed towards a mountain in the far distance.

the Ngorongoro Crater, another extinct volcano,' he
d. 'We're not far from there. About an hour to go.'
cy pressed her face against the window and couldn't
ve how empty everywhere appeared: no towns, no roads,
fields. Kal would call it awesome. She turned from the
dow and glanced at her brother.
Her cry of alarm woke Ellie.
Craig looked up from the newspaper he was reading and
rned in his seat. 'What's the problem?'
The girls were making stuttering noises and pointing at Kal.
'Kal's working the controls; he's, he's…' Lucy couldn't get
the words out.

Craig nodded and went back to his paper.

Kal turned and grinned.

'Keep your eyes on the road!' yelled Lucy. 'The sky, I mean.'
She and Ellie clung to the seats in front.

'We're okay,' said Craig. 'I'm watching him.'

Gradually, Lucy relaxed, and when she realised the tiny plane
wasn't about to fall out of the sky – even with Kal at the
controls – she turned her attention back to the scenery below.

There was very little sign of civilisation except the occasional
hut and one or two dirt roads leading into the distance. Then,
having reached the middle of nowhere, Craig said they'd
arrived.

Lucy saw a small patch of green with a bungalow and some
other buildings. 'Is that Simba?'

'That's it.' Craig took over the controls from Kal and banked
the plane round.

'Fupi, look: Simba,' cried Lucy.

Fupi yawned.

'All right, I know, but this is my first time.'

Lucy nudged Ellie.

Her sister looked up from her book. 'What?'

'We're almost there.'

'Oh, right.' Ellie glanced out of her window.

'Isn't it brilliant?'

'Sure.' Ellie went back to her book.

This is the best thing ever, thought Lucy. Why isn't everyone excited? She shook her head and looked out of the side window. Giraffes! Three of these beautiful creatures were nibbling at the tops of some trees, completely ignoring the plane coming in to land.

She peered over Craig's shoulder as he lined up on a strip of sandy ground beyond the buildings. Some zebras were standing right where they were going to land. Surely Craig had seen them.

He revved the engine and the zebras galloped off.

Fupi yawned again.

'All right, Miss Know-All.'

The plane's wheels rattled on the bumpy ground. Trees and bushes flashed by. The plane rapidly slowed and stopped. Craig switched off the engine and everyone climbed out.

'What a beautiful place,' said Ellie, taking a deep breath. 'The air's so clear, and it's so warm. Thanks for inviting us, Craig.'

'Thanks for coming.'

Lucy lifted Fupi down and she went scurrying off sniffing, but kept coming back to the children, panting and wagging her tail to say welcome to Simba.

'It's just so brilliant,' said Lucy. 'What's that?' she cried, pointing to a black and white bird with a large orange-red beak, bobbing up and down and going *wuk-wuk-wuk-wuk*.

'Red-billed hornbill,' said Craig. 'They're common here on the ranch.'

'My second bird,' cried Lucy.

'Looks like a naff parrot to me,' said Kal.

Craig laughed and pointed into the distance. 'See, there's the hill: Mlima ya Simba.'

'That doesn't look much like a lion,' said Lucy.

'Don't blame me,' said Craig, 'I didn't name it.'

They looked up at the sound of an approaching vehicle, but none of them – not even Kal – had seen a Land Rover like this. The cab and all the windows, except for the windscreen, had been removed. There were dents in the wings and doors, and the paint was falling off. But it wasn't so much the vehicle which attracted their attention, as the driver. He wore a red check blanket over one shoulder. Round his neck was a bead necklace and there was a matching bracelet on his wrist. His ear lobes were greatly stretched by some elaborate bead earrings, and his hair had been braided in long tight plaits and smeared with what Lucy later learned was fat and a kind of clay called red ochre. When he got down from the vehicle, she saw his sandals were made from,…from tyres. Shoes made from car tyres!

'He's a Maasai,' whispered Ellie to Lucy. 'He's awesome.'

'This is Joel,' said Craig. 'He's our head game scout.'

'What's that sort of sword thing in his belt?' asked Kal.

'It's called a *simi*,' said Craig.

'Wicked.'

The only Swahili Lucy had learned was: hello, and she now greeted the smiling man. '*Jambo*, Joel. I'm Lucy.'

'*Jambo*, Lucy. *Habari yako?*'

'Er.'

'That means: how are you?' whispered Ellie. 'You say: *nzuri*, which means: fine.'

'Er, *nzuri*,' said Lucy.

'Very good, Lucy,' said Joel. 'You will soon speak Swahili.'

Lucy grinned. 'Not sure about that.'

Chapter 5

Wildlife Vet

Ever since Lucy heard they were coming to Tanzania, she'd been learning about the wildlife from the books Mum had bought her. She was expecting things to be a bit like home, where she would get all excited if there was a deer on the other side of a field, or if a fox crossed the road in front of the car's headlights, or if she saw a woodpecker in the park. But here! There were so many different animals; they were so close and none of them took any notice of the Land Rover.

She saw monkeys, baboons and warthogs, more giraffes, loads of different-coloured birds, and a small herd of reddish antelopes called impala. It was like being in a zoo – one without bars.

The vehicle came clear of the trees and there before them was a stone and wood bungalow with a brilliant orange creeper cascading over the green tin roof. Chattering sunbirds were searching for nectar among its flowers, the sun glinting on their plumage. In front of the veranda, which ran the length of the house, was a lawn on which two orange and black birds were probing with long curved beaks.

'Hoopoes!' cried Lucy.

'More for the list,' said Craig.

She grinned.

A tall lady came down the steps of the veranda to meet them. She had wrinkly brown skin and wore a flowery cotton dress. Craig's mother, Mrs Elliott, reminded Lucy of Mrs Sandford, their headmistress, but she smelled of wood smoke rather than school dinners.

'Come and have some refreshment, children, you must be tired after your long journey.' She led the way up the steps to the veranda.

'*Come and have some refreshment, children,*' whispered Ellie,

19

copying Mrs Elliott's headmistressy voice, and starting Lucy giggling.

'Hey, what's that?' Kal pointed at a greyish brown animal like a large guinea pig which scampered up the steps ahead of them.

'It's a hyrax,' cried Lucy. 'I've got a picture in one of my books.'

The hyrax regarded them briefly before jumping onto a chair beside an elderly black Labrador which grinned and thumped its tail.

'He's Pimbi, one of my babies,' said Mrs Elliott.

The children looked at her uncertainly.

'An orphan whose mother was killed by an eagle,' she explained.

'Have you got any other orphan animals, Mrs Elliott?' asked Lucy.

'Lucy, you must call me Diana.'

Lucy gulped. Imagine, Mrs Sandford saying: "*you must call me Belinda*".

'Yes, we have quite a collection,' said Diana. 'You can help feed them later if you like.'

'Yes please, Mrs Ellio… Diana, that is.'

A large lady wearing a headscarf, a green dress and a broad smile, appeared carrying a tray with drinks and a plate of biscuits. '*Jambo wote* – hello everyone,' she said. 'I am Martha.'

She put the tray down and her smile broadened as she came and greeted them each in turn. 'You are most welcome.'

'Martha is our housekeeper,' said Diana. 'Her husband, Samson, manages the cattle on the ranch.'

'Why do Africans smile so much?' Lucy whispered to Ellie and Kal.

Ellie shrugged.

'Toad-Face didn't,' said Kal.

'Come on, guys, stop nattering,' said Craig. 'Grab your drinks and some seats.'

Lucy settled back in her chair and gazed out over the ranch. 'This is just so brilliant.'

'We think so,' said Diana.

'Is that a lion?' asked Kal.

'Where?' Lucy leapt up, spilling her drink.

'There.' Kal pointed at a skin lying over the back of her chair.

'Don't do that, Kal.'

'Yes,' said Craig. 'It was killed by a buffalo.'

'A buffalo!' said Kal. 'What happened?'

'It was an old lion forced to hunt on its own and it went for a buffalo calf. But the mum objected.'

'And sorted it?'

'Big time. You don't mess with buffaloes – they can be bad news.'

'Do you shoot dangerous animals, Craig?' asked Ellie.

'No ways. We're a conservation ranch. Besides, animals are only dangerous if you don't respect or understand them. We keep a couple of rifles to take with us in the bush, but we've only had to use them to scare animals off, never to…'

His voice trailed off as a powerfully-built man wearing jeans and a T-shirt hurried onto the veranda and whispered in his ear.

Craig frowned as he listened.

The children glanced at one another.

The man finished talking to Craig and turned to the children. His face broke into a warm smile. '*Jambo*, my name is Samson. Welcome to Simba.'

There was more hand shaking. By now, Lucy's hand was beginning to ache.

'Some men have brought an injured animal,' said Samson. 'They're hoping Craig can treat it.'

'What sort of animal?' asked Lucy.

Craig stood up. 'Let's find out.' He led them through the house and out of the back door.

Two men, wearing similar Maasai clothing to Joel, were sitting on their haunches under a tree. Their spears were stuck in the ground beside them. A sack lay nearby but whatever was inside was keeping very still.

Craig called to them in Swahili.

'*Chui*,' replied one of the men.

Ellie gasped.

'Ellie, what is it?' cried Lucy.

'It's a leopard. They've brought a leopard. Is that right, Craig?'

Craig nodded. 'They say some children saw a young leopard near their goats, and one of them threw a spear. When they wounded it, they got frightened and told their father – he's the taller one.'

'Why were they frightened?' asked Lucy.

'Because they know I'm trying to protect the animals and they thought I'd be angry if I found out.'

Lucy looked at the sack. 'It's not moving.'

'Come,' said Craig. He picked up the sack and led them through a clump of trees to a collection of pens containing an assortment of young animals. 'Our zoo,' he said, waving his hand round the pens. 'All orphans which have been rescued. Most of them arrived in sacks.'

'Your own zoo?' cried Lucy.

'Temporary zoo,' said Craig. 'As soon as the animals are ready, we release them back to the wild in a safe part of the ranch.'

'You've got zebras and warthogs and... What's that?'

'It's a bushbuck. Kind of forest antelope,' said Craig.

Lucy ran across to Joel, who was in one of the pens bottle-feeding a young zebra. 'Can I help?'

'Later,' called Craig. 'I need Joel's help here.' He opened the door of an empty pen and placed the sack on the ground.

Joel joined him and carefully cut open the sack with his *simi*. A beautiful spotted animal lay there not moving.

'A serval!' exclaimed Craig. 'It's not a leopard.'

'It's dead,' said Lucy. 'That is so sad.' She could see a horrible red gash down the animal's chest exposing muscle and bone beneath.

Craig peered into the animal's mouth then felt its chest. 'No, it's still alive – just.' He stood up. 'Lucy, you told me you wanted to be a wildlife vet, now's your chance.'

'What!'

'I'll help. Come in. This guy won't run off.'

22

Lucy entered the pen and knelt beside the serval. She put a hand on its chest and felt a fluttering heartbeat and the occasional gasping breath. 'Please get better,' she whispered.

'I just need to get the gear from the house,' said Craig. 'If he stops breathing, push down on the chest a few times.'

Lucy chewed her lip. 'Don't be too long.'

'Hang in there.'

'Anything I can do?' asked Kal.

'Not yet,' called Craig, over his shoulder. 'I'll be as quick as I can.'

He beckoned to Ellie and they ran back to the house.

Lucy inspected the wound and waved away the buzzing flies. The serval's breathing was very shallow, and every time it breathed out, a little spout of pink froth came from the wound in its chest. She nestled her head against the animal's soft fur. 'Don't die,' she whispered.

Craig came hurrying back. Behind him was Ellie, carrying a bowl of hot water with antiseptic.

'Right, let's see what we can do.' Craig opened a box full of instruments, syringes, bandages and bottles of different medicines. 'Long way from hospital here – we have to be able to deal with emergencies.'

He took out a bottle and drew some liquid from it into a syringe. 'This is local anaesthetic. I know the guy looks peaceful, but we don't want to risk it.'

He passed the syringe to Lucy. 'There you go.'

Lucy was horrified. 'I've never done this before. What do I do?'

'I'll hold the wound open,' said Craig. 'Just squirt a small amount over it. Good. Now put the needle here into the muscles and the skin. Great. Keep going – all round the wound.'

Lucy was concentrating so hard, she didn't have time to think how horrible the wound was, or whether the serval was going to die, or how uncomfortable she felt kneeling in the dirt, or how hot the sun was on the back of her neck.

'That'll do,' said Craig. 'Now while we wait for the local to

23

work, you can clean the wound.'

Lucy picked off some bits of dried grass then washed away the dirt as well as she could.

Craig passed her a sterile swab. 'Put that over the hole to stop the air getting into his chest – that's his main problem.'

Lucy held the swab in place with one hand, and continued cleaning the rest of the wound using her free hand. She remembered programmes she'd seen on television of vets working in spotlessly-clean operating theatres where all the people wore green gowns and facemasks, and were operating on dogs and cats, with names like Fenton or Darcy, which were suffering from ingrowing toenails – not servals with spear-wounds, lying in the dust of Africa.

'Eh? What?'

'Let's see about closing the wound,' repeated Craig, who was holding a curved needle in a pair of forceps.

Lucy removed the swab, and Craig skilfully sewed the two sides of the hole together.

'Looks like he's breathing better,' said Kal, who was leaning over the fence.

Craig peered into the serval's mouth. 'Good. And see, the tongue's looking a better colour.' He passed Lucy a container. 'Antibiotic powder; sprinkle it over the wound before we sew up the skin. It's impossible to work under sterile conditions here.'

He began closing the wound with stitches, while Lucy assisted by holding up the edges of the skin with another pair of forceps. Finally, he passed Lucy the curved forceps and needle. 'You do the last stitch.'

She gulped and tried to remember what she'd seen Craig do. Her stitch wasn't as neat but she was really pleased she didn't make a mess of it.

'Lucy, the wildlife vet,' said Craig.

She quickly brushed the tear off her cheek. She felt really proud.

'Cool, Lucy,' said Kal.

'Lucy, that was really good,' said Ellie.

She blinked a few more times and grinned. 'Thanks, guys.'

Craig injected some antibiotic into the serval's neck. Kal then helped him carry it on the sack to another pen which was fully enclosed.

'They climb nearly as well as leopards,' said Craig. 'We don't want him getting out before we're ready.'

'We need to give him a name.' Lucy wrinkled her brow. 'What's Swahili for serval?'

'Mondo.'

'That's it!'

Craig smiled. 'Good name.'

'Can I stay with him for a bit?'

'Sure. Joel will be around. Give a shout if you need any help. I'll get some water. Trickle small amounts into his mouth. Just make sure he swallows.'

'Okay.' Lucy sat on the ground beside Mondo and gently lifted his head into her lap. To think: my first patient.

When Craig and the others returned an hour later, Lucy and Mondo were in the same position. His eyes were still closed, but he was purring softly.

Chapter 6

Lucy Goes Birdwatching

That night after supper, Martha showed the children to a log cabin a short way from the main house. 'This is called a *banda*,' she said. 'There's a room for each of you.'

'Can I have this one?' asked Lucy, opening a door and peering in. 'What's that net thing over the bed?'

'To keep the mosquitoes away,' said Martha.

'Mosquitoes transmit malaria,' said Ellie.

'Know-all,' muttered Kal.

Fupi, who had followed them, now stood at the foot of the bed looking up at Lucy.

'Are you allowed?'

Martha turned away. 'I'm not looking.'

Lucy quickly lifted up the mosquito net and Fupi jumped onto the bed and wagged her tail.

'You'll get fleas,' said Kal.

'Rubbish,' said Lucy. 'Don't tell Mum, though.'

***

Lucy lay in the dark with her arm around Fupi. 'What a brilliant day, Fupi. All the amazing things we've done. So many different birds and animals and wonderful people. And Craig letting me help with Mondo. I just know he's going to be all right, Fupi. Fupi?'

But Fupi was asleep.

'You're the best of all, though,' she whispered.

Lucy listened to the strange sounds of the night: some were birds, some were mammals, some were insects, some were even frogs, and some were the wind caressing the trees and grass.

She didn't know any of the sounds at the time, but over the next few weeks, she learned to recognise the calls of nightjars, stone curlews, owls, zebras, cicadas and even lions. But on that first night, they were simply sounds – a kind of bush orchestra which lulled her to sleep.

Next morning, the bush orchestra sounded very different –
as though all the birds in Africa were trying to out-sing each
other and wake her up. She could hear Kal's snores coming
from the next room. How could he possibly sleep through that
racket?

There was a knock on the door and Fupi sat up.

Martha entered carrying a mug of tea. '*Jambo*, Lucy, how did
you sleep?'

'*Jambo*, Martha, very well.'

'Lucy, you should say: *nzuri sana*. It means: very well or very
good,' said Martha, setting the mug beside Lucy's bed.

'*Nzuri sana*. How's that?'

'*Nzuri sana*,' cried Martha, clapping her hands. 'Craig wants
to make an early start this morning, and has asked me to wake
you all up.'

'I was awake –it's brill here.'

'Brill?' She seemed puzzled.

'Martha, it's not very good English. It's slang.'

But Martha wasn't listening. As she went out of the room to
call the other two, Lucy could hear her murmuring brill, brill to
herself.

Lucy gave Fupi a hug. 'It really is brill.'

She let Fupi out of the *banda* then had a quick shower, got
dressed and ran across to the main house. Martha was setting
the breakfast table and Craig was in his office at the end of the
veranda talking to someone on a radio – they didn't have a
telephone at Simba and mobile signals were unreliable. He saw
her and waved. She waved back and went to help Martha.

'And how's Lucy today?' asked Craig, coming out of his
office.

'*Nzuri sana*.'

'Hey, man!'

'Martha's been teaching me some Swahili.'

'Great.'

'How's Mondo?'

'Let's go and see.'

27

Lucy followed Craig to the animal pens. She was terrified they might find that beautiful animal stretched out stiff and cold on the ground. Her heart was pounding as she approached Mondo's enclosure and saw him lying on some bedding in one corner.

'Mondo,' she called. 'Mondo.'

The serval put up its head.

'Craig, he's going to be all right.'

'Looks like it. Joel tells me he's already eaten some food. See, and there's no swelling round the wound. You did a good job, Lucy.'

She looked into his face and smiled. 'He looks quite like a leopard.'

'We don't often see them on the ranch, that's why the guys were confused.'

'Would he have killed the goats?'

'Unlikely. They normally go for rodents, but the Maasai children don't understand that.'

'Do the Maasai often attack the wild animals?'

Craig shook his head. 'No ways. Provided their own animals aren't threatened, they leave them alone. I guess this guy came a bit too close. Come on, let's go and get breakfast.'

They returned to the veranda, where Martha had produced a mountain of food, which Kal was fast demolishing.

'Craig, what's happening today?' asked Kal, through a mouthful of bacon and eggs.

'We're going on safari, over there, to the Seki Hills.' Craig pointed into the distance. 'I want to check them out before your dad arrives, but it'll mean spending the night there. You guys all right with that?'

'What, camping?' said Lucy.

'Joel's loading the gear now.'

'Brilliant.'

'Ace,' said Kal.

'But we're going there to work.'

'What sort of work?' asked Kal, a note of wariness in his voice.

28

'A bit of flying and—'

'What!'

'I need to photograph the places we want your dad to survey, so while I'm taking the pictures you can help with the flying.'

'You call that work?'

'Sure.'

'Awesome.'

Ellie arrived. Her hair was spiked up with gel and she wore combat jeans, a T-shirt depicting a pop-star band, and pink flip-flops.

'Great safari gear,' said Kal.

She pretended not to hear.

'We're going camping,' cried Lucy, 'and Kal's going to fly the plane and… and it's the sort of work like Craig does all the time.' She wasn't sure this was strictly true, but Craig didn't say anything. 'Isn't that great?'

Ellie shrugged. 'Whatever.'

'Don't you want to come?'

'I'll see.'

'You're being a wimp,' said Kal.

'No, I'm not!'

'You'll be fine, Ellie,' said Craig. 'But you might, er, want to change your footwear.'

Ellie glared and said nothing. A few minutes later she left the table and went back to her *banda*.

'Is she okay?' asked Craig.

'Don't take any notice,' said Kal. 'She's just trying to be cool.'

'Right, guys, this is the plan,' said Craig. 'The main reason for going to the hills is to build an airstrip.'

'An airstrip?' said Lucy. 'How are you going to do that?'

'We find a flat space, clear a few rocks and bushes, and—'

'And that's it?'

'More or less. We paint some stones to mark it out and use it as our starting point when your dad gets here.' He helped himself to more coffee. 'While Kal and I are taking the photographs, Joel will drive the Landy to another airstrip between here and the hills. Kal and I will then meet him there.

29

What do you girls want to do?'

'If Kal's going to be flying, we'll go with Joel,' said Lucy.

'Fair enough,' said Craig. 'Go and grab your things and, Lucy, bring your binoculars and bird book, then we'll be off. I can hear Joel coming now.'

Lucy and Kal ran back to the *bandas*, and returned with Ellie; now wearing trainers but still looking uncertain.

Lucy was relieved to see the Land Rover was different from the open one Joel had been driving yesterday. This one had a cab and a roof-rack which was piled with bags and camping gear. Kal told her the vehicle was a Defender one-ten long-wheel-base – whatever that meant.

'The one we were in yesterday was a short-wheel-base,' said Kal.

'Oh,' said Lucy, not having a clue what he was talking about.

Fupi wagged her tail and looked expectantly between them.

'Is Shorty coming?' asked Kal.

'Her name's not Shorty,' said Lucy. 'It's Fupi.'

'Same thing. Fupi means "short" in Swahili. Craig told me.'

'I don't care. Fupi's a much nicer name.' She scooped Fupi into her arms and turned to Craig. 'Can she come with us?'

'Of course. Fupi is my nose and ears in the bush; just as Joel is my eyes.'

***

Two hours later, Lucy, Ellie and Joel were sitting on their haunches in the shade of a tree at the end of what Joel assured the girls, was an airstrip. Except for the absence of bushes or trees, the place didn't look to Lucy any different from the rest of the area. Some antelopes, which Joel said were Grant's gazelles, were standing in the middle of it. Lucy sat down with her back to the tree, got out her binoculars, and studied them. They were quite like the impala she'd seen yesterday, but she supposed Joel knew what he was talking about. There wasn't much else to see: a few small brown birds pecking in the dust and Craig's plane in the distance circling round the hills. It seemed to be taking ages.

'What's that mound thing, Joel?' asked Lucy, pointing to

30

what looked like a giant sand castle with holes, one of which Fupi was sniffing.

'It is a house for termites – white ants.'

'An ant-hill. But it's massive.'

Joel shrugged. 'Sometimes mongooses and snakes live in the holes.'

'Snakes!' cried Ellie.

'Don't be pathetic,' said Lucy, getting up to inspect it. 'They're not going to leap out at you.'

'I don't care. You can go and look on your own.'

Lucy looked questioningly at Joel.

'It is safe,' he said.

Lucy peered down some of the holes but saw nothing – not even a termite. By the time she finished her inspection, Ellie and Joel had gone into a huddle and he was pointing out things and telling her their Maasai names.

Lucy wondered what Mrs Sandford would think if we told her that the "educational purpose" for which Mum had got us off the last week of school, involved crouching in the dirt in the middle of Africa with a Maasai warrior wearing a blanket over his shoulder and a wicked-looking sword, called a *simi*, round his waist, and learning a language which was nothing like French. So what?

She gazed around. The gazelles hadn't moved, but beyond them, a large black bird had appeared, striding across the ground. Before Lucy could study it through her binoculars, it walked behind some bushes and disappeared. She got up and crept towards the bushes. The gazelles trotted off. Lucy glanced back at Ellie and Joel, who were still engrossed. Fupi was asleep under the Land Rover.

'I won't be a moment,' she murmured.

The black bird had reappeared but was still striding off. She got a better view this time and thought it looked like a turkey. She stopped and checked her bird book but couldn't find anything about turkeys. The bird continued its purposeful walk. Lucy hurried to get nearer. The bird was now in the open and had been joined by another. She got a better view this time.

The birds were all black and about the size of turkeys, but they had large curved beaks and bright red faces.

She crept behind a bush and checked in her book again. 'They're not storks and they're not cranes.'

The birds moved off and Lucy followed. It was so exciting tracking them.

She settled down beside another termite mound and peered through her binoculars. The birds seemed to have caught something and were tossing it into the air – a lizard or possibly a snake. Poor thing.

Something startled the birds and they flew off, displaying a large patch of white on their wings. She went back to her bird book. 'Here we are: ground hornbills. They're not much like the red-billed one I saw yesterday.' She sighed. 'It's really confusing.'

She couldn't wait to tell Craig.

***

Kal couldn't imagine anything more exciting. Under Craig's watchful eye, he was flying a plane across the African bush. Flying a Tornado was very tame in comparison.

The Cessna had dual controls, and while Craig operated the main set, Kal operated the other, the plane responding to his every movement: turning, banking, climbing. Whatever he did, the plane obeyed him. He felt the g-force when he banked, and his stomach sink when he climbed. He could hear and smell the engine. And he could feel the heat of the sun beating into the cabin. At home, whatever he did to the controls, made no difference to the behaviour of the sofa. But here…

'Nearly there,' said a voice beside him.

Kal came out of his dream. But it wasn't a dream. He looked across at Craig, and grinned.

'How's it going?' asked Craig.

'Wicked.'

Craig winked back. 'See that hill. Fly towards it, then turn and we'll fly a number of transects.'

'Copy that.'

For the next half hour, Kal flew back and forth over the hills while Craig took a series of photographs. He was aware of Craig watching him and giving the occasional instruction, but there were no instances when Kal needed his help.

Craig put his camera away. 'Time to find the others. Over there,' he said, pointing.

A few minutes later, Kal saw the Land Rover at the end of the airstrip. Two figures stood up and waved.

'Do you reckon you can manage?' asked Craig.

'You want me to land the plane?'

'Why not?'

'Cool.' Kal licked his lips, banked the plane round, lined up on the airstrip, and moved the controls gently forward.

The plane dipped and, as the ground came racing towards them, he eased off the throttle and brought up the nose. He glanced quickly across at Craig, who nodded. The plane came lower. Kal held it steady as their speed dropped. He eased further off the throttle. It seemed almost as though the plane was now floating above the ground.

There was a bump, then another, and they were down, with the wheels of the undercarriage rattling over the rough ground. He shut down the throttle and applied the brakes.

The plane coasted to a halt and Kal switched off the engine. 'That was epic.'

'That was excellent,' said Craig. He opened his door and the two of them scrambled out.

'Where's Lucy?' called Craig, as Ellie and Joel came to greet them.

'She's just...' Ellie looked around. 'She was... Oh no!'

Chapter 7

Ant-lions

Lucy packed away her binoculars, picked up her bird book and got to her feet. She shaded her eyes and scanned the hills where Craig and Kal had been flying, but couldn't see the plane. *Were* those the hills, though? She gazed around. Or, perhaps it was the hills to her left. They looked very similar. She thought she could hear a plane but couldn't tell where the sound was coming from.

'This is silly,' she said to herself. 'Anyway, it doesn't matter. I ought to get back to Ellie and Joel now.'

She set off towards the termite mound from where she'd watched the hornbills. When she got to it, it didn't look quite right. This one had a hole at its base – a large hole with flies buzzing in and out.

She backed off. Whatever had made the hole was still inside.

She tried to re-orientate. *There* was the termite mound. That was the one.

When she reached it; it wasn't.

She began to feel uneasy.

'There's nothing to worry about,' she said out loud. Hearing her own voice gave her reassurance. 'I'll navigate by the sun, like they tell you in books.'

The sun was directly overhead.

'Hmm. What about tracks, then? I'll follow my tracks and retrace my steps.' She peered at the sandy ground. She couldn't even see her tracks. The sand was so soft and dry that her footprints were just blurs amongst countless other blurs.

She sat down. 'Come on, Lucy, the important thing is to think – the others can't be that far away.'

She picked up a twig and began to draw in the sand. 'If the airstrip is here, and the hills where Craig and Kal were flying are here; that means I came this way.' She drew a line in the sand.

'So I must be about—'

Something threw sand at the twig.

She started back then peered down.

Nothing.

Something must have fallen from above. But there wasn't anything above, except blue sky and cotton-wool clouds. She must have imagined it. She went back to her drawing. 'That means I'm—'

There it was again. This time there was no doubt. Something was throwing sand at her twig – something hidden in the ground. Then she noticed little pits in the sand all around. It was when her twig went near one of these that a spurt of sand was thrown at it. She had no idea what it was.

'Anyway,' she said, getting up, 'I'm not wasting any more time. Craig will know.'

She checked her drawing, glanced around, saw the direction she should be heading and strode off. 'Five minutes – ten, at the most.'

She kept checking her watch. Twenty minutes later, there was no sign of the plane, or Craig, or Ellie, or Kal, or Joel, or Fupi. But she knew she was heading in the right direction. She began to run.

Something snorted and crashed off through the bushes ahead – something big.

She stopped. She couldn't see what it was but she could still hear pounding. Was it hooves? Or was it her heart?

She slumped against a termite mound. She'd given up wondering whether it might be the one she was looking for. She closed her eyes and waited for her breathing to settle. Then tears started. She began to realise how hot it was, how similar everything appeared, how she had no water, and how she was… how she was completely and utterly lost.

She cupped her hands round her mouth. 'Ellie.'

A bird flew out of a nearby tree but there was no answering cry.

'Ellie! Ellie, where are you?' Her cries were swallowed up in the bush. There wasn't even a reassuring echo from the surrounding hills. It was like pouring water into sand.

'ELLIE.'

Another bird – or perhaps the same one – started calling, as though mocking her.

She collapsed to the ground and let the tears flow. 'Ellie, Kal, where are you?'

She was lost, she would die of thirst and vultures would eat her body. She had sometimes wondered what dying would be like. She'd never imagined it would be like this.

Pounding feet. That animal was coming back. Nowhere to hide. This was it!

She covered her head with her arms and hunched herself into a ball.

The animal was upon her. Snuffling round her head. Trying to get at her face.

'Get away!'

The animal barked.

Her mind began to register.

'Fupi?'

She sat up.

'Fupi!'

The little dog leapt into her arms and covered her face with a frantic slobbery tongue.

'Oh, Fupi.'

'Are you all right, Lucy?' said a voice.

There was Joel, smiling and breathing hard.

'Yes.' She didn't care he could see she was crying.

***

'I guess I don't need to say anything,' said Craig, looking down at Lucy, who was slumped with her back against a wheel of the Land Rover, sipping tea.

The others were standing round her.

'No,' she said in a small voice. 'Craig, I'm really sorry.'

'We were so worried,' said Ellie.

'You could have been eaten by a lion,' said Kal.

Lucy sniffed and nodded as she sat hunched over the mug cradled in her hands.

'Five more minutes,' said Craig, 'and I would have taken the plane up to search for you.'

Lucy gave a weak smile. 'I'm glad you care about me,' she said, and burst into tears.

'Oh, Lucy!' cried Ellie, kneeling down and hugging her. 'Of course we care about you.'

Lucy sniffed then blew her nose. 'How did Joel and Fupi find me?'

'The best trackers in Africa,' said Craig.

'You made a very good path,' said Joel, 'but you were going.' He waved his hands around in circles.

'Lucy, it's so easily done,' said Craig. 'You keep thinking you recognise a twisted tree or a strange-shaped termite mound. The trouble is, all the trees are twisted and all the termite mounds are strange shapes.'

'I know.'

'If it should ever happen again – and heaven forbid – orientate by the wind. That's one thing which tends to be constant here, always blowing from the same direction.'

'I'll try and remember,' she said, then perked up. 'But I did see some ground hornbills.'

Craig shook his head. 'Lucy, you're a case.'

She grinned. 'And something funny in the sand.'

'What?' asked Kal.

'Like sort of… Look, there. Those pits.'

'Ant-lions,' said Craig, 'or rather the larvae of ant-lions. Fupi'll show you.' He pointed to one of the pits. 'Go, Fupi.'

She sniffed where Craig was pointing and began to dig. In no time, she scooped out a wriggling creature with large jaws which immediately tried to rebury itself.

Fupi went to pounce on it, but Craig held her back.

'These things live in pits like this for a number of years,' he said, 'and anything such as an ant, which comes near, gets a face full of sand which knocks it into the pit. It slips down the side and into the jaws at the bottom.'

'Wicked,' said Kal.

Joel located an ant and steered it towards a pit with a stick. A puff of sand was thrown up. The ant slipped in. There was a brief flash of jaws and the luckless ant disappeared.

'Pow!' cried Kal.

'What do they turn into?' asked Lucy.

'Rather beautiful creatures like dragonflies which fly at night.'

'Are they dangerous?' asked Ellie.

'Not at all. They're one of what we call the little five.'

'I've heard of the big five,' said Lucy, now fully recovered from her ordeal.

'Okay, Lucy, what are they, then?' said Craig.

'Um. Lion, leopard, rhino, elephant and… and hippo.'

'Almost right: elephant and buffalo,' said Craig. 'The big five – what every tourist hopes to see.'

'I think the hippo should be on the list,' said Lucy, 'then it would be the big six.'

'I agree, but I'm afraid it's the big five – and the little five.'

'It's a wind-up,' said Kal.

'No ways – they're all real animals. You've got the ant-lion; then there's the buffalo-weaver, rhinoceros-beetle, elephant-shrew, and leopard-tortoise.'

'Leopard-tortoise?' cried Kal. 'What does that do, climb trees and jump on animals?'

Craig chuckled. 'Not quite; tortoises don't—'

A frantic bark from Fupi made them look up. A whirling roaring cloud of sand and dust was rushing straight at them.

'Quick!' yelled Craig. 'You kids, all on the tail of the plane, shut your eyes, and hang on like crazy.'

They raced to the plane. Craig and Joel each grabbed a wing and the children clung to the tail. Fupi dived under the Land Rover. They watched in horror as this great monster – over a hundred metres high – roared towards them, throwing leaves, sticks, sand, and the occasional bird, into the air. Then it hit them, pounding with stinging particles of sand and tugging clothes and hair.

The plane bucked and kicked like a wild horse trying to break free.

Lucy kept her eyes screwed tight and tried to hold her breath while clinging on. She needed to breathe. Still the stinging pounding roaring sand. How much longer could she hang on? How much longer could she hold her breath?

Chapter 8

Elephants Won't Charge

The tornado was over as suddenly as it started. Lucy cautiously opened her eyes and blinked, trying to get the gritty sand out. 'That was scary.'

Fupi shook herself.

'What was it?' gasped Ellie.

'Dust devil,' said Craig. 'Well done, you lot – that could have been bad news if we hadn't held the plane down.'

'I won't be able to get clean for a week,' said Ellie, trying to rub the sand out of her gelled hair.

'Who cares?' said Kal.

'Typical!'

They watched the dust devil weaving its crazy way across the bush before it petered out some way off in the distance. Craig called for Joel's help and between them they fixed anchor ropes to the wings and tail of the plane in case another one should come through.

'Right, guys: a snack,' said Craig. 'Then we should get going.'

They sat in the shade of a tree and munched slices of watermelon, the juice running down their chins.

Craig said the tree was called *Cordia* because you could use fibres from it to make cords or ropes. Joel, though, said his people called it Seki, and that's how the hills got their name. Then Craig said, in South Africa, they called it snot-berry – which appealed to Kal. Lucy found it very confusing.

Joel murmured something and pointed with his chin. An enormous antelope, like a large sandy cow with twisted horns, was watching them. Fupi pricked up her ears and kept very still.

'What is it, Craig?' whispered Lucy.

'Eland. Isn't he magnificent? Largest antelope in Africa.'

Ellie gave a whimpering squeak.

The animal snorted, tossed its head and was gone.

Lucy couldn't believe such a large animal could simply vanish. She wondered if that was what she'd frightened – or rather – what had frightened her.

They finished their snack and Craig packed the things back into the Land Rover. Ellie went to climb inside.

'It's more fun on the roof,' said Craig. 'Lots to see.'

'Is it safe?'

Kal gave her a withering look, scrambled onto the bonnet and then the roof, where he settled down amongst the camping things.

'You get a great view,' he called.

Ellie and Lucy followed.

Craig passed Fupi to Lucy then climbed up beside them.

'Okay, Joel?' he called. '*Tuende* – let's go.'

Driving cross-country was very slow because Joel had to keep changing direction to go round rocks or trees, or avoid gullies, but gradually the hills crept nearer revealing patches of forest on the top.

Craig tapped on the roof of the vehicle and Joel stopped.

'Is this it?' asked Lucy.

'Not yet.' Craig pointed to the side. 'Look there, just beyond those trees.'

'I can't see any— Wow, elephants!'

'They look awfully big,' said Ellie. 'Will they charge?'

'No,' said Craig. 'They're used to vehicles. See, they're taking no notice. If we were on foot we'd have to be more careful.'

He leaned over the edge of the roof. 'Drive a bit closer, Joel.'

'Please don't go too close,' said Ellie.

'It's okay, Joel's taking us down wind,' said Craig.

'What does that mean?' asked Lucy.

'The wind will blow our scent away from the elephants so they won't smell us.'

Joel stopped about fifty paces away and switched off the engine.

The elephants were completely wild, yet here they were, having elevenses, and apart from raising their trunks to try and sniff the visitors, taking almost no notice of the vehicle or the

41

people on top.

'They've got indigestion,' said Kal.

'That rumbling noise, you mean?' said Craig.

'Sounds like Dad after he's had curry.'

'Kal, don't be so rude,' said Ellie.

'It's their way of communicating,' said Craig, 'saying they're content – like purring in a cat.'

'Some cat!'

'Why are they reddish?' asked Lucy. 'I thought elephants were grey.'

'That's the dust,' said Craig. 'Murram – the stuff we use here to make the roads. The elephants blow it over themselves.'

'Ellie does that,' said Kal. 'Says it dries the pores.'

'I most certainly do not! Anyway, it's talcum powder, thank you very much.'

'Same thing.'

'Like you'd know!'

Lucy studied the elephants through her binoculars. 'I make it nine.'

'It's a family group we know well,' said Craig. 'They spend most of their time on the ranch. That one in the front with the tatty ears – she's probably about fifty – she's the matriarch—'

'*You must call me Diana,*' mimicked Ellie.

Lucy and Kal burst out laughing.

Ellie turned bright red. 'Oh no!' She put her hand to her mouth. 'I'm so sorry, Craig.'

He grinned. 'I won't tell anyone.'

The elephants flapped their ears but otherwise continued to ignore them.

'As I was saying before I was so rudely interrupted,' continued Craig, 'she's the matriarch; her name is actually Belinda—'

'Oh no!' cried Lucy. 'That's our headmistress.' And she and Ellie started off again.

'When you two have quite finished—'

'They've got the same sort of ears,' spluttered Ellie.

'The old elephant in the front is in charge of the herd,' said

42

Craig, choosing his words carefully.

Lucy could hear occasional sniggers from Ellie and didn't dare look.

'It's a group of females and youngsters,' continued Craig. 'The males leave the herd when they become adult and go off and do their own thing.'

'Don't blame them,' said Kal. 'If I was—'

Joel started the engine and muttered something.

'What did he say?' asked Lucy.

'Moshi!' cried Craig.

'What's that?'

'Trouble. Hold tight!'

Fupi dived down amongst the tents.

'Go, Joel, go!'

Joel slammed the Land Rover into gear, spun the steering wheel and tore off.

The vehicle bumped and lurched over the rough ground. Those on top clung to the roof rack, the camping gear, anything they could grab hold of.

'What is it?' screamed Lucy.

'Behind you!' yelled Craig.

Lucy turned, and there was the most enormous elephant she could have imagined. Its ears were flat against its head and its trunk was tucked back. It was no more than twenty paces behind.

And it was catching them.

Lucy whimpered then gasped as the branches of a low tree raked across the roof.

'Faster!' she screamed.

The Land Rover hit a bump.

Kal yelled and Craig just managed to grab him before he rolled off. 'Hang on!'

They were now on smoother ground and Joel was getting away. But the elephant wasn't slowing. How could such a large animal run so fast? All its attention was focused on the vehicle, determined to destroy it and everyone in it.

They came into an area of low bushes, and Joel had to keep

swerving round them. The elephant, though, crashed straight through – like some enormous tank. Once more, it was gaining on them.

'No-o-o,' wailed Lucy.

Without warning, the elephant stopped, raised its trunk and gave an ear-splitting blast.

Joel didn't slacken his speed until they were a good two hundred metres clear. Then he brought the Land Rover to a cautious halt but kept the engine running.

The children were shaking, and Ellie was whimpering.

'Sorry about that,' said Craig. 'I didn't notice Moshi at the back of the herd.'

'I thought you said they wouldn't charge,' said Lucy, her face still white. She looked back at the elephant which was weaving its body from side to side, flapping its ears and questing with its trunk trying to pick up their scent.

'We haven't seen her for ages,' said Craig. 'Joel spotted her just in time.'

'What if he hadn't?' said Kal.

'Let's not think about it.'

The elephant thrashed the bushes with its trunk, gave a final blast of trumpeting then turned and disappeared into some trees.

'I knew I should have stayed behind,' said Ellie.

'I don't understand it,' said Craig. 'She used to be so peaceful; now she's really bad news – that's why Joel christened her Moshi.'

'What does that mean?' asked Kal.

'Smoke. You never know how it will behave.'

'That figures.'

'Why is she like that?' asked Lucy.

Craig sighed. 'I wish I knew. We'll have to warn the Maasai, though, otherwise someone might get hurt – or worse.'

'Isn't there something you can do to make her better?'

'Sadly, there isn't.'

Lucy looked away so the others couldn't see her sad face.

Joel switched off the engine, climbed out of the vehicle and peered at something on the ground. The others watched as he walked a short way into the bush, still staring at the ground. He then returned and spoke in a low voice to Craig.

'Hang on here a moment, you guys.' Craig jumped off the roof and followed Joel into the bush.

'You're not leaving us?' cried Ellie.

Craig waved. 'Won't be a moment.'

'Please don't be long.'

'What were they talking about, Ellie?' asked Kal.

'Something about tracks I think, but they were talking Maasai and I couldn't really follow.'

Craig and Joel returned looking pensive. Craig climbed back onto the roof, and they continued their drive.

The children watched him, deep in thought.

'Were they some sort of tracks?' asked Kal.

'What? Oh yes. They were… were eland. We don't normally see eland in this area.'

Lucy glanced across at Ellie, who gave a slight shake of her head.

Chapter 9

Searching for Diamonds

They continued their journey in silence, the Land Rover climbing steadily. Finally, they came onto a plateau which overlooked the plain below. Above them, wispy clouds shrouded the summits of forested hills. Craig called a halt and they clambered off the roof, feeling stiff after their bumpy ride.

'That elephant was so scary,' said Ellie.

'Let's have some lunch, take our minds off things,' said Craig. 'Over there, in the shade.'

They sat dangling their feet over the edge of a gully while they munched sandwiches which Martha had prepared for them, and watched the birds coming to feed on the blossoms of an acacia tree on the opposite bank. Fupi sat close by Lucy, waiting to snap up any crumbs.

'These sandwiches are good,' said Lucy. 'What's in them?'

'*Kuku*, I guess,' said Craig.

'Cuckoo!'

'Yuk!' Kal spat out a mouthful. 'I'm not eating flaming cuckoo!'

'Don't be so pathetic,' said Ellie, 'don't you two know anything?'

'What's that supposed to mean?' said Lucy.

'*Kuku* is Swahili for chicken.'

'Craig, why didn't you say?' said Lucy.

He chuckled. 'Eat up, guys, we need to make a move. Kal, can you drive the Landy?'

Kal grinned. 'Dunno, but I'll give it a go.'

'I'm not going in the Land Rover if Kal's driving,' said Lucy.

'Nor me,' said Ellie.

'Good, because I want you girls to go with Joel and do some geology,' said Craig.

'I don't know anything about geology,' said Lucy.

46

'I don't know anything about geology either, that's why I've asked for your dad's help. But let's see if we can give him a start.'

'How?'

'You and Ellie, go with Joel. Look for places where stones have been washed out of the rocks and settled in gullies, as well as collecting bits of exposed rock. That'll give your dad an idea of what's here.'

'Do you think we'll find diamonds?' asked Lucy.

'Lucy in the sky with diamonds? Dream on.'

Lucy grinned. What was wrong with dreaming?

Craig gave Joel a backpack to carry water and plastic bags into which they could put the rocks.

'Either of you girls any good at maths?' he asked.

'I'm useless,' said Lucy.

'Ellie?'

'All right,' she said cautiously.

'Have you seen one of these before?' Craig took something like a mobile phone out of a case.

Ellie shook her head.

'It's a GPS receiver.'

'A what?'

'A global-positioning-system receiver – it receives satellite signals and tells us where we are on the earth.'

'Our coordinates,' said Kal.

'All right, Mr Know-All.'

'Switch it on here,' said Craig. 'Wait for a few seconds and then read off the numbers. As Kal says: the coordinates. Whenever you collect a sample, write down the details. Here, use my notebook. You reckon you can do that?'

'Yeah, no sweat,' said Ellie.

Craig grinned. 'Right, on your bikes. See you later.'

Lucy and Ellie watched a nervous-looking Kal, sitting in the driving seat of the Land Rover listening to Craig.

The engine started with a roar and a cloud of smoke shot out of the exhaust pipe. Then the engine stopped. A few moments later, it started again – this time without the noise and smoke –

47

and the vehicle edged jerkily forward. It reminded Lucy of the way her granny crossed the road.

There was a call from Joel.

The girls, remembering their mission, joined him and Fupi who were in a gully poking around in some stones.

They collected some brown stones, some black and white ones, and some greenish ones, but no diamonds. The stones didn't look very interesting but Lucy supposed Dad would think they were. Ellie recorded the position and Lucy wrote it down on a piece of paper and put it in the bag. They followed the gully to its end, collecting as they went. When they emerged, they were on the edge of the forest. Lucy looked back. The Land Rover was now charging up and down the plateau flattening grass and bushes. Kal and machines.

Lucy tried to tell herself they were doing scientific research, but if this was what science was about, it was pretty boring. They'd now collected a ton of stones – which fortunately Joel was carrying – but they were all dull and uninteresting. She'd long given up hope of finding diamonds.

Something shot out of a bush and ran off.

Lucy jumped.

Ellie squawked.

Fupi stood quivering.

'What was that?' cried Lucy.

Joel pointed towards a bush about fifty paces away, and there was a most beautiful antelope – but it was tiny, no more than half a metre high – standing in the shade of the bush watching them with large eyes and whiffling a long soft nose.

'What is it, Joel?'

'*Diki diki.*'

'A dik-dik! It's beautiful.'

Fupi was like a coiled spring.

Lucy knelt down beside her. 'Good girl.'

Fupi jumped up and licked her face then transferred her attention back to the dik-dik.

'Look. There's another,' whispered Ellie. 'On the other side of the bush.'

48

They watched the two little antelopes for a while then Joel glanced at the sun. 'We must be returning.'

'Wait!' cried Lucy. She dropped to her hands and knees, and peered at something on the ground. She picked it up.

'Look at that,' she breathed, passing a small piece of rock to Ellie.

Ellie held it up to the light. 'It's red,' she murmured. Her hand flew to her mouth. 'Ruby!'

'And here's another bit!' cried Lucy.

All three of them were now on their hands and knees, scrabbling and searching amongst the loose rocks.

Fupi felt she too had to help and started digging furiously.

When they stood up, they were covered in dust, their fingers were scratched and their nails broken, but they were grinning.

'Brilliant!' cried Lucy.

'We must record the coordinates for Dad,' said Ellie. She switched on the GPS receiver and wrote down the figures. 'Let's go and show the others.'

They raced back to Craig and Kal, who were busy painting rocks to mark out the new airstrip.

'We've found rubies!' called Lucy.

'What?' cried Craig. 'Let's see.'

They stared, fascinated, at the small heap of stones, all of which had bits of red embedded in them.

Craig picked one up. 'I can't believe it,' he said, 'and just lying on the surface?'

'Is it ruby?' asked Lucy.

Craig examined another piece. 'We need your dad to confirm it, but it certainly looks like it to me.'

'The ranch is saved!' cried Lucy.

Chapter 10

The Camp in the Forest

Joel drove a short way to the edge of the forest and they set up camp.

When Lucy and Ellie finished putting up their tent, Lucy glanced round to make sure they were out of earshot. 'Did you make out any more, Ellie, about what Craig and Joel were talking about?'

'What, when they went off into the bush together?'

'Yes.'

'Lucy, they weren't talking about eland – I'm sure they weren't. Joel told me the Maasai word for eland is *osiruwa*. I would have recognised it. I think they were talking about people.'

'What sort of people?'

'I'm not sure, possibly poachers.'

'Poachers!'

'Sh! Yes.'

'Could it be anything to do with the trouble that policeman talked to Craig about, when we were at the hotel?'

'I don't know but it could explain why Craig and Joel looked so serious.'

'Ellie, what's going on? And why doesn't Craig tell us?'

***

Ellie had volunteered to be in charge of the food, and now they were sitting round a campfire watching her fry steak. Fupi was lying with her head on her paws, her nose twitching at the smell.

Kal and Joel, who had been filling the Land Rover with petrol from jerry cans carried on the vehicle's roof, came and joined them.

'Aagh!' screamed Ellie, and leapt away from the fire nearly upsetting the frying pan. 'What's that?'

'Mind our supper!' cried Kal.

'It's only a scorpion,' said Craig.

'Only a scorpion!'

'Wicked,' said Kal.

'He won't hurt you, as long as you leave him alone.'

'I could have been killed!'

'He could give you a nasty sting but it wouldn't be fatal,' said Craig.

'That's really comforting!'

Craig flicked the scorpion away with his boot. 'He was probably in one of the logs we put onto the fire.'

'Yikes!' yelled Kal, and leapt out of his seat. 'I've just been bitten!'

'*Siafu*,' murmured Joel.

'Ow!' yelled Kal, frantically brushing at his shorts. 'I'm being eaten alive!' He raced over to the Land Rover and leapt inside.

The others could hear him shouting and cursing. 'They're flaming ants! Ow! One's just bitten—'

Ellie joined in the laughter.

'It's all right for— Ouch!'

Craig hurried over to the Land Rover, found a tin of insect spray, and gave it to Kal. Then he came back and shone his torch on the ground. 'There, see. Watch where you put your feet.'

Lucy and Ellie looked at a line of brown treacle. Lucy peered closer. 'They *are* ants. Millions of them!'

'*Siafu* – safari ants,' said Craig, 'Kal was unlucky enough to put his chair on top of their column.'

Joel moved their chairs to the other side of the fire.

'What happens if they come into the tents?' asked Ellie.

'They're heading away,' said Craig. 'We'll be okay.'

Ellie didn't look convinced. 'I'm keeping the insect spray with me.'

Kal reappeared, fully clothed. 'I could have been ruined for life.'

'You do make a fuss,' said Lucy.

'It's all right for you! You didn't see the size of their jaws.'

'Okay, okay, so you got bitten by an ant.'

'I bet you'd make a fuss, if one latched onto *your* privates.'

'You'll live.'

Ellie sat with her feet tucked under her. 'You never told us we were all going to be eaten alive, Craig.'

'I don't think so.' Craig smiled. 'Ellie, let me tell you I'm far more scared in London than I ever am out here; all that traffic rushing about, the crush in the underground, and all those people – that frightens me.'

'That's different. There are no dangerous wild animals there.'

'People scare me more than animals. But as I said, animals are only dangerous if you don't understand or respect them.'

'What about Moshi?' said Lucy. 'She could have, could have…'

'Sure, she was dangerous, but she behaved normally for an angry elephant. Why she was angry; *that's* what I don't understand.'

'Do you think she—?'

'Hey, what's that?' Kal pointed at something fluttering in the light from the gas lamp.

Craig rose from his chair and caught the insect in his cupped hands. 'There's your ant-lion, Lucy.'

'It's beautiful; those lovely wings. It really does look like a small dragonfly.'

Kal and Ellie crowded round.

'That's really cool,' said Kal.

Coming from him that was quite a compliment for something which wasn't mechanical.

Craig opened his hands and the insect fluttered off into the darkness.

'*Chakula tayari*,' called Joel.

With all the excitement, they hadn't noticed he'd taken over the cooking.

'Food's ready,' said Craig.

Joel served up steaks with bread rolls, roasted sweet corn, tomatoes and bottles of cold drinks.

The children each took a plate and a bottle and settled into their chairs.

'This is what picnics ought to be like,' said Lucy.

'Brirrmpph,' said Kal, his face stuffed with roll.

'Disgusting,' said Ellie.

'Brilliant,' said Kal, when he'd emptied his mouth.

After the meal, Ellie insisted on doing the washing up, and Kal did the drying-up – without even being asked. Then they settled down round the fire, sipped their drinks straight from the bottle, and stared into the embers.

'You all right now, Ellie?' asked Craig.

'I suppose so. It just takes a while to get used to things.'

'Bit different from home,' said Kal.

'You guys are doing really well,' said Craig.

They lapsed into silence for a while then Joel got up. 'Good night,' he said, disappearing into the darkness.

'Good night,' they chorused.

'Where's Joel sleeping?' asked Lucy.

'On top of the Landy – he doesn't like tents,' said Craig.

'Can I sleep there?' said Kal.

'No ways. I've put your tent there, next to the girls.'

'Where are you sleeping?'

Craig pointed to a camp bed with a mosquito net draped over it set on the far side of the clearing. 'I guess I'm like Joel, but I do find the roof of the Landy a bit too hard.' He got up and put another bit of wood on the fire.

'Isn't it brilliant about the rubies,' said Lucy.

'We mustn't get too excited until your dad confirms it,' said Craig.

'But he will. I know he will.'

They sat staring into the fire. It was like being inside a magic bubble of flickering red and yellow light, surrounded by darkness.

'Craig, can I ask you something?' said Lucy, taking a sip from her bottle.

'Sure.'

She poked a log in the fire with her trainer, and watched the sparks rise into the night and mingle with the stars. 'You

53

remember when we stopped this morning, just before we got here? You and Joel weren't talking about eland, were you?'

Craig looked up. 'Why do you say that?'

'I think you were talking about people.'

'Hmm.' Craig stared back into the fire.

'Was it people?' asked Ellie.

Craig nodded.

'Poachers?'

'I don't know. All Joel could make out was the tracks of some men who had recently passed that way.'

'Could they have been poachers?' asked Kal.

'Possibly. But we haven't had trouble from poachers for a while.'

'Could it be linked to that trouble you and Reuben were talking about?' asked Ellie.

'Hey!' cried Craig, 'I really will have to watch what I say.'

'Who's Reuben?' asked Lucy.

'Who's Reuben!' cried Kal. 'He only won the Olympic—'

'He's that really good looking policeman we met at the hotel,' said Ellie.

'Oh, him,' said Lucy.

'*Could* it be linked, like Ellie says?' asked Kal.

'Possibly.'

'Tell us,' said Lucy.

'Okay, but keep it to yourselves.' Craig set his empty plate down. 'We've thought for some time there might be valuable minerals on the ranch and—'

'And now we've found them!' cried Lucy.

'It certainly looks like it. But unfortunately, other people have also heard about the minerals, and they'd like to get there first.'

'What sort of people?' asked Kal.

'Greedy people.'

'But surely this is Simba land,' said Ellie.

'I know, but boundaries are difficult to define out here. We don't have any fences, and the only boundary markers are watercourses and tracks. It's very easy for people, if they want to make trouble, to dispute whose land is whose.'

'Is that why you spoke to Reuben?'

Craig nodded. 'He's agreed to keep his ear to the ground.'

'Do you know who's making trouble?' asked Kal.

'I wish we did,' said Craig. 'Only a handful of people know about the possibility of the minerals.'

'Like who?'

'Samson and Joel know, but they wouldn't tell anyone. Some of the other men who work on the ranch may know a bit, but nothing much. And the management board; they oversee the running of the ranch – they had to approve my inviting your dad here. Then there's you lot. And that's about it.'

'You can trust us,' said Kal.

'I'm sure I can,' said Craig with a smile.

'Who's on the board?' asked Ellie.

'The Minister of Environment and Conservation – he's a good guy – a couple of neighbouring farmers, some Arusha businessmen, the local MP, the American Ambassador – she does a lot helping to raise US funds for us – and our solicitor James Msolla. I don't see any of them causing trouble.'

Craig rose to his feet. 'Anyway, guys, enough of that. Time for bed. Early start tomorrow.'

'Do we need to put the plates and things away?' asked Ellie.

'No, they'll be fine; just leave…' Craig's voice trailed off.

'What is it?' said Lucy.

He didn't reply. Fupi was also listening and whining quietly.

'Is there something out there?' whispered Lucy. 'It's not those men, those poachers?'

He turned back. 'No, no it's nothing. I was imagining things.'

'Are you sure we're safe?' asked Ellie.

'No worries.' He scraped some sand over the fire to damp it down. 'See you in the morning.'

'Come on, Fupi,' said Lucy, and the little dog trotted after her. By the faint light of the moon, she saw Kal disappear into his tent. Then she noticed Craig take his rifle out of the back of the Land Rover before crossing to his camp bed.

She followed Ellie into their tent, but didn't tell her about the rifle. Besides, Craig probably always kept it with him at night. She didn't bother to change into her pyjamas but wriggled down into her sleeping bag. Fupi crawled in and snuggled against her. It was Lucy's first night in the African bush but she didn't feel afraid despite what they'd talked about. She knew Fupi would warn them if anything, or anyone, came in the night. And Joel was on the roof of the Land Rover, and Craig had his rifle – and they'd found rubies. Everything was, was…

She was asleep.

Chapter 11

Encounter in the Forest

Lucy woke next morning, unzipped the flap of the tent and peered out. Craig, Kal and Joel were sitting by the fire warming their hands on mugs of tea and chatting.

Craig saw her and waved.

She returned the wave then slipped back into the tent. Her clothes from yesterday smelled of wood smoke, but having slept in them, she wasn't going to change them now. She put on her trainers, and she and Fupi joined the others by the fire, leaving Ellie still asleep.

'Sleep okay?' asked Craig.

'Like a log.'

'I knew you would.' He passed her a mug of tea.

'Thanks.' She settled down beside them and let the magic of the cool morning wash over her. Apart from the occasional crackle from the fire, the only sounds were birdsong – no doors slamming, no people calling, no traffic noise, no radios blaring, no aeroplanes overhead. It was wonderful.

'What's that bird?' she asked, pointing to the top of a large tree from which musical whistling notes were coming.

'Black-headed oriole,' said Craig. 'Look! There it goes.'

Lucy saw a flash of golden yellow as the bird flew to another tree and resumed its calling. 'What a beautiful call.'

'Another one for the list?' said Craig.

She nodded.

'By the way,' said Craig, 'did you guys take a mug into the tent last night?'

'No.' Lucy shook her head. 'I don't think so. Why?'

'We had a visitor in the night.'

'What sort of visitor?'

'One that collects mugs.'

'Some animal?'

'They don't normally go off with mugs.'

'You mean a person?'

'Joel thinks so. He's found some tracks and is going to follow them up.'

'Can I go?' asked Kal.

'No ways. We're staying here. We'll decide what to do when Joel gets back.'

'Will it be safe?' asked Lucy. 'Sorry, I'm beginning to sound like Ellie.'

'Who is?' said a voice. And there was Ellie peering out of the tent and blinking like an owl in the early morning light.

'Nothing,' said Lucy.

'You were talking about me.'

'We were wondering how you could still be asleep on such a beautiful morning,' said Craig.

Ellie grunted and disappeared back into the tent.

'Craig, don't say anything about what's happened,' whispered Lucy. 'You know how worried Ellie can get.'

'Sure.' He turned and spoke to Joel, who went over to the Land Rover, pulled out a spear with a blade like a razor and disappeared into the forest.

Craig crossed to his camp bed and returned with his rifle, which he laid beside him.

***

They finished breakfast, and Ellie and Lucy had just taken down their tent, when they saw Joel was back.

Craig waved for the girls to join them. 'We're going hunting,' he said. 'You up for it?'

'What do you mean?' asked Ellie.

'You'll see. Follow Joel, but don't get too close. I'll come at the back.' He fitted a lead to Fupi's collar and she looked most disapproving. 'There you go, Lucy.'

Lucy took the lead and tried to smile.

Craig picked up his rifle and called to Joel.

There was no time to feel afraid as they followed Joel along a narrow game trail into the forest: Kal first, then Lucy and Fupi, and then Ellie, who wanted to stay close to Craig at the rear.

It was much cooler and darker here, and it took a while for their eyes to adjust to the gloom. They jogged gently downhill, trying to be as quiet as possible, dodging round trees and ducking under branches.

Joel held up his hand and they stopped.

Fupi wagged her tail uncertainly and glanced up at Lucy.

'We must be going slowly and be very quiet,' whispered Joel.

He crouched low and crept forward.

The others followed.

When they reached the top of a slope, they lay down and peered over.

Joel pointed to what appeared to be a thick bush. He grasped his spear and began to advance. Kal was now almost on his heels, with Fupi just behind straining against the lead and Lucy struggling to hold her back.

Then Lucy realised it wasn't a bush, it was some sort of shelter.

Joel pointed with his spear at a heap of skins inside.

A poacher's den!

One of the skins moved.

Lucy put her hand over her mouth – too late to stop the scream.

Fupi barked.

The skins erupted and something leapt up.

Lucy saw two frightened eyes.

A skinny body shot out of the shelter.

There was a tussle, and Joel hissed as a set of teeth sank into his arm. Then he was sitting on top of a dirty boy, pushing his face into the ground.

Fupi was still barking and it was all Lucy could do to hold her back.

Joel was now laughing despite the blood running down his arm. But the boy looked terrified.

'Who is it?' asked Ellie, sounding as if she'd got something stuck in her throat.

'Our night-time visitor, I suspect,' said Craig, coming out of the shelter with the missing mug and a bundle of wire snares.

Fupi was now growling and curling her lips.

'He's a poacher?' said Lucy

'Seems like it.'

'Look, over there,' cried Lucy. 'It's a dik-dik – like we saw yesterday.'

Craig went and examined it. 'It's been tied up.'

'Is it a pet?' asked Lucy.

Joel murmured something.

'Joel thinks it's the boy's dinner,' said Craig.

'No!'

Craig untied the animal and carried it over. 'Lucy, I think one of his back legs is broken.'

'We can't leave him.'

'So what do we do? It's only a youngster; if we let him go he'll get chomped.'

'I'll look after him.'

'Are you sure? It'll be a lot of work and he may not survive.'

'I don't care.'

Craig sighed. 'Okay, another for the zoo, then.'

He took Fupi's lead and placed the baby dik-dik into Lucy's arms. It blinked its large round eyes and sniffed her clothes with its whiffly nose.

'Craig, he's so beautiful. I'm going to call him Caspar.'

'Why Caspar?'

'He's my pet cat – we had to leave him behind in England.'

'Why do you want to name him after that old rat bag?' said Kal.

'He's not a rat bag! The least we can do is remember him.'

'Caspar it is, then,' said Craig. He turned to the boy who was now sitting up. Joel had twisted his arms behind his back to stop him running off.

'Now, Sunshine,' said Craig, 'what are we going to do with you?'

Fupi gave an extra growl as if to say: 'Think about that, Buster.'

Craig and Joel both tried talking to the boy, but he just stared ahead, apparently not hearing them. Suddenly, he began to shake and his eyes rolled up into his head.

Fupi started barking again.

'Craig, he's sick!' cried Ellie. 'We must help him.' She grasped the boy's shoulders. His shaking subsided and his eyes came back into focus, but he was still very frightened.

Joel spoke to him and pointed to Craig, who gave a savage growl, which Fupi repeated.

'Okay, Joel, let him go,' said Craig.

Joel hauled the boy to his feet. He appeared to be about Kal's age, but was terribly thin and dirty, and he had a horrible open sore on his leg around which flies were feeding. Fupi sniffed it and the boy cringed away.

'Hey, what's this?' Kal, who had been poking around in the shelter, held up a small bag made from the skin of some animal. The boy gave a cry, and would have rushed forward if Fupi hadn't growled.

'And look here,' said Kal, showing them a small bow and some arrows.

'Don't touch those arrows!' shouted Craig.

Kal froze. 'What is it?'

'Let me see.'

Kal held out the arrows.

The boy's eyes darted between him and Craig.

'Probably *Akocanthera*,' said Craig, studying a sticky black paste smeared on their tips. 'It's a poison made from the roots of a bush which grows round here.' He dabbed a finger on the paste and cautiously licked it. 'Fresh. I guess there's enough poison on this arrow to kill an elephant.'

'Wicked.' Kal held the arrows as though they were red-hot and looked at the boy in admiration.

Joel took the arrows and wrapped them in one of the skins from the shelter.

'What's in the bag?' asked Craig.

'A few old stones.' Kal passed the bag over, and Craig tipped the stones onto his hand.

'They don't look very interesting,' said Ellie. 'Like those we collected yesterday.'

'Well, let's see what your dad makes of them,' said Craig. He asked the boy a question, but he didn't respond.

When they were back at camp, Joel gave the boy some bread and a cup of milk. It was as though he hadn't eaten for ages. He then relaxed a bit but still refused to answer any questions. He just stared ahead of him.

'What are we going to do with you?' said Craig, looking perplexed.

The boy continued to stare.

'Let me talk to him,' said Ellie. 'He's terrified of you two. He's convinced either you're going to shoot him or Joel is going to spear him.'

'I doubt you'll have much joy,' said Craig. 'He won't understand English and probably not much Swahili either.'

'That's all right; I'll try him in Maasai.'

Craig shook his head in disbelief.

'Joel's been teaching me.'

While Ellie went to talk to the boy, Joel and Kal finished packing up the camp and loaded the Land Rover.

Craig and Lucy examined Caspar.

'Is his leg broken?' asked Lucy.

'Seems like it.' Craig gently felt it. 'Probably when he was caught in one of our friend's snares.'

'Will he be all right?'

'We should be able to fix it.' Craig went to the Land Rover and came back with his medical box. He borrowed Joel's *simi* and cut two bits of stick from a nearby bush, then with Lucy's help, bound the sticks against Caspar's leg with sticky tape, being careful not to make the dressing too tight.

Caspar struggled but Lucy was sure he knew they were trying to help, because when she told him his new name and what they were doing, he relaxed, whiffled his nose and blinked his eyes.

Craig found an empty box in the back of the vehicle. Lucy placed her sweater in the bottom and put Caspar on top. Then she collected some fresh leaves and offered them to him. He sniffed them suspiciously at first but then started to nibble.

'Don't forget he has to go back to the wild,' said Craig.

Lucy said nothing; then she whispered in Caspar's ear. 'I'm going to look after you.'

He seemed to understand because he whiffled his nose again. It was a rubbery sort of nose which could bend round corners. It was really cute.

Craig and Lucy went to join Ellie and the boy, who was eating another piece of bread.

'How's it going?' asked Craig.

'He won't tell me his name, Craig, but he says his home is over there.' Ellie pointed into the distance. 'He doesn't want to go back because he says he'll be beaten.'

'We can't leave him here – besides that wound needs treatment.' Craig bent down and examined the boy's leg. 'Hmm, not good.' He fetched his medical box and began to clean the wound.

'Ugh, that is so gross!' cried Lucy, and almost threw up. 'There are maggots in it.'

'They look horrible,' agreed Craig, 'but they probably helped to keep it free of infection.'

When Craig had finished, Joel helped the boy get clean and Kal gave him some of his spare clothes. He now seemed more cheerful and actually smiled.

'Okay, let's go,' said Craig. 'We're taking him home. Joel knows—'

'But he'll be beaten,' cried Ellie.

'I'm sorry, Ellie, but he can't carry on living like that in the forest. It's the best thing for—'

'Please, can't we—?'

'We've got to take him back.'

'But if what if—?'

'Ellie, there's no alternative.'

'Why won't anyone listen to me?' She stormed off across the clearing and stared into the forest.

Craig winced. 'We're going, Ellie,' he called to her back. 'Let's get it over.'

Ellie made no move.

'We'll pick you up on the way home,' called Kal.

Ellie turned, ran back to the Land Rover, jumped inside and slammed the door.

Lucy could see she'd been crying. She climbed in beside her sister and put her arm round her. 'Craig knows what he's doing,' she whispered. 'It really is the best.'

Chapter 12

Lucy Speaks her Mind

Ellie and Kal sat in the middle seats in the Land Rover with the boy between them, and Lucy sat in the back to make sure Caspar didn't scrabble out of his box. They drove mostly in silence, although Ellie, with some help from Joel, kept talking quietly to the boy.

They joined a track about half an hour after leaving their campsite and continued driving on it for nearly an hour before coming to a fork.

'We're going left here,' said Craig. 'This is where we leave the ranch.'

Soon after, a settlement came into view, which Joel said was called a *manyatta*. It consisted of a circle of low huts made out of sticks and mud, the roofs of which the women covered in cow dung when the rains came.

'Why do women get all the rubbish jobs?' said Lucy.

'It's because— Ouch!' cried Kal, as Lucy jabbed him from behind.

There was an untidy broken fence of thorn branches round the shabby huts, and the only thing new, was a shiny vehicle parked under a nearby tree. Some women were sitting on the ground scraping a cow skin, while scruffy children with flies over their faces, crawled among them. The whole place was really sad, and Lucy had the feeling something was very wrong. She wasn't surprised the boy was unhappy. In fact, he looked terrified.

Craig switched off the engine.

Some dogs barked, their hackles rose and they walked towards the vehicle on stiff legs.

Fupi glared at them and growled.

Joel put his head out of the window and called to the women. They looked up without interest. Then one of them rose and went into the nearest hut.

Joel got out of the vehicle and waited.

'What's happening?' asked Lucy.

'Joel has asked to see the owner of the *manyatta* – a man called ole-Tisip,' said Craig. 'I don't know the guy, but Joel says he's bad news.'

'The place looks a bit of a mess.'

'I'm surprised; the Maasai people normally keep their *manyattas* very tidy.'

'I said we shouldn't have come here, but no one listened,' muttered Ellie.

'I'm sure I've seen that Range Rover before,' said Kal.

'There are plenty of Range Rovers around nowadays,' said Craig.

'Yeah, but I bet there aren't too many silver V8 supercharged Vogue SEs like that.'

'True.'

'It *is* the one!' insisted Kal. 'The one Toad-Face and Rat-Man were in.'

'I thought they were in a space ship,' said Ellie.

'Get lost!'

'Are you sure you didn't imagine it?'

'No, I didn't! The owner was short and— That's him! That's Toad-Face.'

Two men emerged from one of the huts. One was tall and wearing an army greatcoat, Wellington boots and a woolly skiing hat. Funny place to go skiing, thought Lucy. The other was fat and wore a suit.

'That *is* him!' cried Kal. 'The one in the suit – I'm sure it's him.'

'You're right,' cried Lucy. 'He was at the hotel.'

'Good grief,' said Craig. 'It's Gideon Nagu, our local MP. What did you call him?'

'Toad-Face. Because he's got sticky-out eyes and a mouth like a letter-box.'

'I bet he's the one who nicked Dad's briefcase,' said Kal.

'What's he doing here?' asked Lucy.

'I've no idea,' said Craig. 'Do you recognise the other guy, Kal?'

'Not sure. He's the right height but he was like wearing this T-shirt with a rat on it and I didn't really notice his face.'

The two men whispered to each other as they studied the visitors, then they approached the Land Rover.

'Hang onto Fupi,' said Craig, getting down from the vehicle. 'And stay here.'

The boy didn't need any encouragement. He was crouched on the floor.

'*Jambo*, Craig,' called Toad-Face, a phoney smile on his face.

'*Jambo*, Gideon,' said Craig, as he shook the man's hand. 'How are you?'

'Fine, fine.'

'What brings you out here?'

'A social call – you know how it is. Just visiting my old friend, ole-Tisip.'

The other man said nothing and made no attempt to offer his hand. Instead, he was holding a kind of club thing and slapping it against his leg.

'What's he holding?' whispered Lucy.

'It's called a *rungu*,' said Ellie.

'I bet that could do some damage,' said Kal.

'So, my friend?' Toad-Face put an arm round Craig's shoulder. 'Is yours also a social call?'

Craig said something the children couldn't hear. Then the tall man started shouting and waving his arms.

The boy crouched even further down on the floor.

'Can you understand what he's saying, Ellie?' said Lucy.

'He's talking about the boy.'

'Shouting more like. What's he saying?'

'He's saying the boy is bad. He seems to be blaming him for the fact that cows have been dying, and that's why his place is in such a mess.'

'That's not fair,' cried Lucy. 'And Craig certainly doesn't think so.' She could see he had his arms folded across his chest and his mouth was shut tight, as the man ranted on.

'Craig has told him the boy's sick and needs treatment. Hang on, that tall man said something about being the best thing if he died.'

'What!'

Before Ellie could stop her, Lucy jumped down from the vehicle and ran over to the men.

Fortunately, Kal was holding Fupi's collar or she would have followed.

'He needs help – he's sick!' shouted Lucy. 'You can't say he should be left to die!'

The man couldn't have been more surprised than if she'd just teleported from Planet Zorg. His mouth dropped open, showing stained brown teeth, and he was dribbling.

'I think you're horrible! And if I was him, this is the last place I would want to live!'

The man clearly didn't understand a word Lucy was saying, but Toad-Face did, and he looked just as startled.

'Well, well, who's this?' he managed to say. He had a silly squeaky voice and his smile had now gone. Lucy didn't like the look which replaced it.

'I'm his friend,' she shouted.

Tears were starting in the back of her eyes, but she wasn't going to let *them* see. 'And he's coming home with us!'

'Come on, Lucy, let's go.' Craig put his arm round her shoulder. He said something to the two men, and led her back to the Land Rover. Joel followed.

***

Lucy sat in the front between Craig and Joel with Fupi on her lap. No one said anything as they drove away. Then Craig said in a quiet voice: 'That was very brave, Lucy. I was proud of you.'

She couldn't hold back the tears any longer.

'Lucy, you were brilliant,' said Ellie. Then *she* started.

'I'm so sorry,' Lucy sniffled, as Fupi licked her face. 'Craig, I didn't mean to cause trouble. I was so—'

'You've probably just saved the boy's life.'

She sat up – the tears forgotten. 'What?'

68

'It seems his parents are both dead—'

'He's an orphan?'

'Yes,' said Craig. 'And no one was prepared to look after him.'

'That's awful!'

'So, without treatment, he would probably have died there, or more likely run away again and died in the bush.'

'Can't he stay with…? I mean can he come with…?' She couldn't say the words.

'Can he come with us?'

'Yes. That is…'

'I was about to tell ole-Tisip what I'd decided, when you, young lady, arrived on the scene and expressed rather more forcefully what I was about to say.'

'So he *can* stay with us?'

'For a while, anyway.'

'Yes!'

'Is he going to be okay?' asked Kal.

'His leg needs treating, but I reckon we can do that back home. If not, I'll take him to hospital.'

The boy was now sitting up trying to follow their conversation. Although he couldn't understand what they were saying, he obviously knew they were talking about him. Then Joel explained and the boy seemed very pleased.

Lucy grinned at him and he gave an uneasy smile.

'He reminds me of the ant-lion,' said Ellie suddenly.

'Oh yeah,' said Kal.

'It's true. Before, he was hiding in that dark place in the forest and now he's come out into the open, like into a new life – like the ant-lion.'

Joel was laughing.

'Why's that funny, Joel?' asked Lucy.

Joel made snapping movements with his fingers and pointed to the wound on his arm. 'That one has the teeth.'

'He's got to tell us his name now, Joel.'

Joel spoke to the boy then chuckled. 'He says is name is Matata.'

'What does that mean?'

'It means trouble. It's what his mother used to call him.'

'What's his real name?'

'It is a difficult Maasai name – even for me.'

'Matata it is, then,' said Craig.

'Like the song from *Lion King*,' cried Ellie '*Hakuna matata* – no worries, no problem.'

'Let's hope so,' said Craig.

Ellie and Lucy began to sing.

There was a sudden shout from Kal. 'Caspar's escaped!'

'Craig, stop!' Lucy jumped out and ran round to the back door of the Land Rover.

Caspar had climbed out of his box and managed to get himself stuck between two bags.

Lucy lifted him clear, and he whiffled his nose as if to say thank you.

***

They returned to Craig's plane and, while he and Kal flew back, Joel drove the rest of them to the house.

When they arrived, Craig introduced Matata to Martha, who made a great fuss of him and took him to her own house.

Lucy helped Craig remove the temporary splint from Caspar's leg and set it in a plaster bandage. Then they put him in the pen with a baby eland. Although the two were very different in size, they sniffed each other's noses and immediately became friends. Lucy could see that the eland – whose name was Pofu – was explaining to Caspar everything that went on at Simba. Afterwards, Caspar found himself a quiet corner in the pen and sat with his eyes half-closed pretending to be asleep. He didn't seem at all frightened. It was as if he'd always lived there.

***

They'd just finished dinner that evening on the veranda, when Martha appeared twisting her apron in her hands. 'Please, Diana, it's the boy, Matata.'

'What's the matter with him?'

'Has he run away?' cried Lucy.

Martha shook her head. 'No. It's just that… it's…'

'What, Martha?' asked Diana.

'God has told me I won't have any children of my own and…' Her apron twisting became more agitated.

'Go on, Martha,' said Diana.

'Now Matata has come… and he has no home … and I… that is Samson and me, we could look after him… and he could live with us… and we could feed him … and he wouldn't be any trouble… and we would make sure he was a good boy… that is if…' She was now looking at her feet, but still working her apron. 'Would you and Craig let Matata stay with us?'

Diana glanced at Craig and then at Martha.

Lucy looked at Ellie and Kal, not daring to say a word.

'Does he not have any family?' asked Diana.

'His parents are both dead,' said Martha. 'He had a sister but she died. That man, ole-Tisip, wouldn't pay for her to get medicine.'

'He's so awful!' cried Lucy.

'Have you said anything to the boy?' asked Diana.

Martha continued to stare at her feet. 'He would be very happy. He says the *wazungu* children and Craig and Joel are very kind.'

'What does Samson say?'

'He says it is God who has brought Matata to us.'

Diana sat thinking for a moment. 'Well,' she said slowly, 'we could do with some help with the orphan animals when Lucy leaves, and—'

'Yes!' Lucy leapt up and gave the startled Diana a huge kiss.

Ellie and Kal grinned.

'I'm sure he'll be very happy with you,' said Diana.

Martha wiped her eyes on her apron; then a big smile broke across her face. 'That's brill.'

'That's what?' said Diana.

'That's brill.' Martha looked uncertain.

'Where on earth did you learn that word?'

Martha turned to Lucy, who had gone bright red. 'From Lucy.'

71

'I see.' Diana paused. 'Yes, well, I suppose it is rather brill.'

Everyone laughed.

'An orphan to help with the orphans,' said Craig. 'Sounds good to me.'

'Splendid,' said Diana. 'Why not bring him through, Martha.'

A few moments later Martha returned with Matata. He was looking squeaky clean and very nervous. There was a clean bandage on his leg and he was wearing... Kal's England-football shirt!

'Kal, that's your favourite shirt,' whispered Lucy.

'But I've got loads of shirts; he hasn't got any.' Kal looked embarrassed.

Chapter 13

A Dangerous Confrontation

At the end of the week, Craig flew to Arusha to collect Mum and Dad. When he returned, he buzzed low over the house to announce their arrival.

Kal called Lucy and Ellie when he heard the plane, and the three of them piled into the open Land Rover, which Kal was now allowed to drive, and sped off to the airstrip.

Craig taxied to meet the waiting vehicle, and as soon as he switched off the engine and opened the door, the children rushed forward.

'Mum, we've found rubies, and the ranch is going to be—'

'And Craig and I have been flying—'

'And I've got this beautiful little dik-dik; it's a kind of antelope—'

'And we rescued this boy called Matata, but that's not his real—'

'And Craig says we can—'

'It's so lovely to see you all,' cried Mum, hugging them each in turn. 'Look at you.'

With all the time they'd spent in the open, Kal's hair was getting bleached, Ellie's spots had disappeared, Lucy's nose was peeling because she always forgot to put sun cream on it, and all of them were tanned.

'You look so well.'

Dad climbed out of the plane and joined them. 'How are you kids? Having a good time?'

'Yes thanks, Dad,' they chorused.

'Did you find your briefcase?' asked Ellie.

'I'm afraid, it hasn't turned up, but the hotel has promised to keep an eye open for it.'

'I still think Toad-Face nicked it,' said Kal.

Lucy could contain herself no longer. 'Dad, we've found

73

rubies.'

'Are you sure?'

'Positive.'

'Well, that is good news.'

They looked up at the sound of another vehicle arriving, with Joel in the driving seat and Matata and Fupi beside him.

'The driver is Joel and that's Matata – the boy we rescued,' said Ellie.

'Which boy?' said Mum.

'The one we were telling you about.'

'Were you?'

'Mu-u-um! The boy we rescued from the forest.'

'Yes, dear. He's wearing a shirt like Kal's.'

Ellie quickly explained.

'Kal, that's really generous.'

'No sweat.'

Mum gave a slight start.

Lucy thought that Kal was sounding more like Craig every day. He'd told her he wasn't trying to copy Craig's accent, it just happened that way. She didn't believe him.

Craig produced a new football he'd bought in Arusha and booted it across to Kal. 'Go and teach Matata to play.'

Kal trapped the ball then flicked it onto his head and bounced it a few times, while Matata watched in amazement.

'Here, Mat.' Kal kicked the ball across. Matata stopped it with his foot and kicked it back, but it spun off his toe and shot off to the side.

'Like this,' called Kal. He demonstrated, and Matata returned a perfect pass.

'Shouldn't we be getting on?' said Dad. 'Work to do.'

'Yes, sure,' said Craig. 'Okay, guys, bring the ball. You can practise on the lawn.'

He put the bags in the back of Joel's Land Rover. 'David, would you mind going with Joel and Matata?'

'Not at all. There's a bit more room in that one.'

'The rest of us will go in the other vehicle.'

'Fine. See you at the house.'

'You're not letting Kal drive, I hope?' said Mum, as they climbed aboard.

'Why not?'

'Well I… he's not… he doesn't… He hasn't passed his test.'

'He has with me.'

'But shouldn't you be sitting beside him?'

'Why?'

'Well… in case he…'

'In case he what?' Craig was smiling.

'In case— Nothing! Come on, Kal, what are we waiting for?' She turned to the girls. 'Isn't this wonderful?'

'It's brilliant!' cried Lucy.

As Kal followed the track through the trees, the animals were as plentiful as on Lucy's first journey. 'Mum, it's like being in a zoo – only better.'

Mum was still smiling in bewilderment as they emerged from the trees, and the house lay in front of them.

'Mum, see all the birds,' said Lucy. 'Those orange and blue ones, making all that noise, are superb starlings, and there's a scarlet-chested sunbird – or maybe a Hunter's, they're very similar. And those ones on the lawn are hoopoes, and those are masked weavers, and—'

'Lucy, Lucy,' cried Mum, 'I can't take it all in.'

'Craig's been teaching me the names of all the different birds. I'm making a list and I've already recorded over a hundred.'

'That's marvellous.'

Kal pulled up, and Diana came hurrying down the veranda steps and embraced Mum. 'Lovely to see you again, Sarah, after all these years. How long has it been?'

'Certainly before the children were born.'

'My, how time flies.' Diana led the way back up the steps. 'Welcome to Simba.'

'Grab some seats,' said Craig, pushing some chairs forward after the various animals on them had been shooed off.

'Nice spot this, Craig,' said Dad, who had arrived ahead of them. 'I was studying the geology as we flew in. It appears that the main formations are pre-Cambrian with volcanic intrusions, probably quaternary.'

'Like I said,' murmured Kal, glancing at Lucy, who started to giggle.

Dad ignored them. 'I imagine you still have some seismic activity in the area.'

'We get the occasional earth tremor, but nothing serious,' said Craig.

'Rock falls – that kind of thing?'

'Yes, and once the kitchen door jammed.'

Dad nodded. 'I would expect that. Now, from a mineral perspective, the main areas of interest will probably be at the margins where intrusions have pushed up through the basement rock.'

'Exactly.' Kal had his hand over his mouth.

Craig winked at him, and tried to follow what Dad was saying.

'Take those hills there, for example—' Dad pointed into the distance. '— they could be a promising place to start.'

'Those are the Seki Hills,' cried Lucy, 'where we found the rubies. Ellie's recorded the coordinates on Craig's GPS – that's a global positioning system.'

'Yes, Lucy, I am familiar with the technology.'

'Oh. I just thought— '

There was a rattle of crockery, and Diana and Ellie appeared carrying the lunch trays.

'Come and sit down, everyone,' called Diana.

'So, Craig, what's the plan?' asked Dad, as soon as they were settled.

'I thought we'd spend today here. Let you relax a bit. Then tomorrow we could fly over the Seki Hills, and other parts of the ranch, and you can decide which areas you want to look at from the ground.'

'That sounds fine. Good plan.'

'Sarah, would you like to come?' asked Craig.

'I'd love to.'

'Kal?'

'Yeah, sure.'

'But you'd better not do the flying tomorrow,' whispered Craig. 'Your parents might get worried.'

'Sure.'

'In the meantime, Craig,' Dad said, 'perhaps I could examine the samples you've collected. Was there something about rubies?'

'I'll go and get them,' said Lucy and rushed off.

As soon as the lunch table was cleared and the others were having coffee, Dad took a field microscope from his bag and began examining the rocks.

Lucy sat on the edge of her seat trying to keep still. 'Are they rubies, Dad?'

'Lucy, do be patient,' said Mum.

'Yes, but are they rubies?'

Dad turned away from the microscope. 'No, Lucy. I'm sorry to say they're not rubies.'

Lucy crumpled. 'Not rubies! But those red—'

'They're garnets.'

'What are they?' Lucy slumped back in her chair. 'So much for research!'

'A form of calcium or magnesium aluminium silicate – probably common in the area. But what I find so interesting is—'

'Are they valuable?' asked Kal.

'They have some trivial value.'

The children sat looking dejectedly at each other.

Craig got up. 'Anyone for more coffee?'

They all shook their heads.

'I guess it's back to the drawing board, then,' said Craig.

***

Mum had been to her *banda* and changed, and was now back on the veranda. Craig and Dad were examining the other rocks which had been collected. Kal and Matata were playing football, and Diana had gone into the house to talk to Martha about dinner.

Ellie and Lucy pounced on Mum and started telling her everything which had happened. They were just getting to the bit about the *manyatta* when Kal came racing up the steps looking hot.

'That man's come.'

'What man?' said Craig.

'Toad-Face.'

'Do you mean, Gideon Nagu?'

'Yeah, if that's his name. He wants to talk to you, Craig.'

'Where's Matata?' asked Ellie.

'He legged it as soon as he saw who it was,' said Kal.

'Who is this person you're talking about?' asked Dad.

'He's horrible,' said Lucy. 'He's all podgy and has a really creepy voice – and he has a mouth like a letter-box.'

'A what?'

'His name is Gideon Nagu,' said Craig. 'He's a member of our management board, and also happens to be our local MP.'

'Really, Lucy,' said Dad. 'You should be more respectful. This is a good opportunity to meet him. It's important to be on good terms with such people.'

'Dad, he's a creep.'

'Lucy, that's quite enough!' said Mum.

'Ah, Craig my friend.'

Lucy recognised the squeaky voice and turned to see the man come puffing up the steps of the veranda.

'Good afternoon, Gideon,' said Craig, getting to his feet. The two men shook hands.

Fupi growled and Toad-Face looked uncertainly at her.

'Is that one safe?'

'As long as I'm here,' said Craig.

The man backed away.

Dad hurried forward. 'Good afternoon, sir, I'm Dr David Bartlett. Craig has called me in as a geology consultant. I'm very pleased to have this opportunity to meet you.' He shook the man's podgy hand.

The man seemed a bit surprised but quickly put on his phoney smile.

'Good afternoon, doctor, are you enjoying your visit?'

'Yes, very much. I've only just arrived, but I have reason to think there could be some promising mineral deposits in those hills over there.' He pointed in the direction of the Seki Hills.

'Is that so – promising in what way?'

'Well, I haven't had a chance to see things from the ground but aerial inspection suggests that—'

'David,' said Craig, 'I don't think we should raise expectations at this stage; not until you've had a chance to visit the site.'

'No, perhaps you're right.' Dad turned back to the man. 'I do apologise, sir, my enthusiasm sometimes gets the better of me.'

'Please don't apologise. What you tell me, doctor, sounds most interesting. Those hills, you say?'

'Actually, Gideon,' said Craig, 'Dr Bartlett and I must have been talking at cross-purposes. The material came from that escarpment.' He pointed in a different direction.

'But I thought you said it was from—'

'Can I offer you some tea or coffee, Gideon?' asked Craig.

'No, I won't stay. I came about the boy.'

'What boy?'

'The boy you brought to my friend's *manyatta* the other day, when you were with the charming English children – so spirited.'

'Creep,' muttered Lucy.

'What about him?' said Craig.

'My friend ole-Tisip apologises about the misunderstanding. He will be very happy to look after the boy. So, I've come to take him back.'

'You can't!' cried Lucy.

'Charming, charming,' murmured the man.

'No, Gideon,' said Craig quietly. 'He is happy here.'

Lucy wanted to rush up and hug him.

'But this is not his home.'

'It is now.'

'Craig, we should discuss this. It would be better for the boy to grow up in his traditional environment.'

'Sorry, Gideon, there is nothing to discuss.'

'I'm only thinking what is best for the boy.' The phoney

smile was disappearing fast.

'So am I, Gideon. He stays.'

'I think you're being very short-sighted.'

'Gideon, the boy stays here. He's being cared for by my assistant manager and his wife.'

'You, my friend, are being very foolish.' He glared at Craig then turned and went down the steps. He climbed into his vehicle and put his head out of the window. 'You can expect to hear more from me.'

'What a dreadful man,' said Mum, as he drove off.

'He was perhaps a bit forceful,' said Dad. 'But I respect that in a man.'

'Dad!' cried Lucy.

'Do you think he'll make trouble?' asked Mum.

'No.' Craig shook his head. 'I know he's on the board, but he's not as important as he thinks.'

But Lucy could tell he was only saying that so Mum wouldn't worry.

Craig turned to Dad. 'David, I apologise for interrupting you, but I think the fewer people who know about things the better at this stage.'

'Absolutely. But the man *is* an MP.'

'Yes, and he has some rather dodgy friends.'

Chapter 14

The Skin Bag

'Dad,' said Ellie, when they had recovered from the unwelcome visit, 'apart from garnets, what else did we find in the hills?'

Dad's eyes lit up. 'Well, the more interesting samples are probably metasomatic with corundum and hornblende inclusions – possibly zoizite—'

'You what?' said Kal.

'Let me finish! Zoizite, or zoizite-amphibolite, occurs in metasomatic rocks, schists and gneisses. These probably comprise the more interesting components of those hills.'

'Interesting!'

Dad gave Kal a withering look. 'A form of zoizite, known as tanzanite, gets its name from this country.'

'I've heard of that,' said Craig.

'Tanzanite can be quite valuable, but what may be significant in these samples are the traces of corundum.'

'Grinding powder?' said Craig.

'Exactly.'

'Grinding powder! And that's it?' said Lucy.

'Yes, Lucy, that is it. Geologically, though, the samples are extremely interesting and I look forward to examining the area tomorrow, but in terms of valuable deposits, I fear we may be disappointed.'

'What about the stones which Matata had in his bag?' asked Kal.

'No!' Craig clapped his hand to his forehead. 'I forgot all about them.'

'Craig, you didn't leave them?' cried Lucy.

'No ways, they're in the door of the Landy.'

'I know,' said Kal. He raced off, and was back a few minutes later with the skin bag.

Craig opened it and tipped out the contents.

'Hmm,' said Dad. 'Now these *do* look interesting – probably from alluvial deposits.'

'What are loovile deposits?' asked Lucy.

'Alluvial! Really, the ignorance of this family.' Dad gave a deep sigh. 'It's where stones are washed out by water and get deposited in hollows and gullies.'

He picked up one of the stones and set it under his microscope. He adjusted the light and began humming tunelessly to himself as he examined the stone, using different lenses and lighting arrangements.

'What is it, Dad?' asked Ellie.

Dad didn't hear her. He picked up another stone and carried on humming. He examined five more stones, and when he finally looked up his eyes were shining.

'I'm pretty certain they contain trigonal prismatic forms of corundum.'

'More grinding powder, then?' said Kal.

'In the granular form, yes, but in the form we have here it is better known as, as ruby.'

Kal said a word, which had Mrs Sandford heard she would have put him in detention for a week. They were all so stunned that not even Mum thought of telling him off.

For a moment, there was silence; then they all started to talk at once.

'So we're rich and—'

'Do you think Matata knows what they—?'

'David, are you sure you—?'

'Can we go back there and—?'

'Good heavens, what's going on?' said Diana, emerging from inside the house. 'You look as though you've just seen a ghost or something.'

'Diana, it's rubies – you're going to be rich!' cried Lucy.

'How nice, dear.'

'Mother, it's true,' said Craig. 'David says some of the stones Matata had with him, contain traces of ruby.'

'Possibly sapphire as well,' added Dad.

'Good Lord.' Diana had to sit down.

'Probably of gem quality,' said Dad. 'But I would like to get a second opinion. Someone like Professor Wafula at the University of Nairobi in Kenya would know.'

'Dad, I thought sapphires and rubies were different,' said Ellie.

'I'm glad you asked that, Ellie.' Dad beamed. 'Sapphire and ruby are both forms of corundum but contain different colouring pigments: normally chrome for ruby, and iron and titanium for sapphires, the colouring depends on—'

'Not another geology lecture,' groaned Kal.

Dad scowled.

'And these stones were found on the ranch?' said Diana.

'We need to ask Matata,' said Craig, 'but I'm assuming they were.'

'No wonder old Toad-Face was interested,' said Lucy.

'Who?' said Diana.

'Lucy means our local MP,' said Craig.

Diana raised her eyebrows. 'I thought I heard a vehicle. What did he want?'

'He wanted to take Matata away.'

'Whatever for?'

'He said he thought it would be best if he grew up in his traditional environment.'

'Craig, though, told him like where he could shove it,' said Kal.

'Really, Kal!' said Mum. 'Where on earth did you learn an expression like that?'

'From Dad.'

'I'm quite sure you did not. I'm also sure that Craig said nothing of the sort.'

'Well, it was something like that. Perhaps he said—'

'That's quite enough!'

'You did ask.'

'Kal!'

'Okay, okay.'

'Toad-Face looked really cross,' said Lucy.

'Craig, do you think he knew Matata had those stones with

83

him?' asked Ellie.

'Could be, but one thing's for sure, he wasn't interested in Matata's welfare. He was…' Craig tapped his chin. 'I think it's time I had another word with Reuben. But first I'll talk to Matata, and find out where he found the stones.'

'Craig, let me talk to him,' said Ellie. 'You'll frighten him. He'll think he's done something wrong.'

'Fair enough.'

Ellie stood up. 'Kal, do you want to come?'

'I won't be much help. I can't understand much of what he says.'

'No, but you're his friend. He'll be more relaxed if you're there.'

Fupi, sensing something was about to happen, jumped off Lucy's lap and ran after them.

***

'It took us ages to find Matata,' said Kal, when he and Ellie returned. 'In the end, it was Fupi who found him hiding in some bushes. He thought Toad-Face had come to take him away.'

'He was right, there,' said Lucy, 'but what did he say about the stones?'

'At first he pretended he didn't understand what I was talking about,' said Ellie, 'but then I said the fat man knew about the stones and had come to take them.'

'What did he say to that?' asked Craig.

'He got very frightened and said his father had given them to him to look after.'

'His father? Did he say why?'

'He said his father was afraid, that's why he gave him the stones.'

'And soon after that his father died,' said Craig. 'Do you know how he died?'

'I didn't ask.'

'Does Matata know where the stones came from?' asked Lucy.

'He tried to tell me but I couldn't really understand what he was saying,' said Ellie. 'It sounded like *mahali pa mfupi ya kichwa*, which sort of means: the Place of the Short of the Head, but that doesn't make sense.'

'Soft in the head, if you ask me,' said Kal.

'Are you sure you got it right, Ellie?' said Lucy.

'I made him repeat it several times. Then he got all upset, so I had to stop.'

'What does it mean, Craig?' asked Kal.

'More or less what Ellie says, but there must be something else to it.' Craig frowned. 'I wonder, what.'

Lucy tried to think. It was like when Mrs Sandford asked her difficult sums such as the square root of eighty one, or what was seven by nine. She knew she knew the answers, but they got stuck in a jumble of numbers and she could never find the right one.

'Think,' she whispered to Fupi, sitting on her lap. Fupi wagged her tail and Lucy could tell she was thinking because her ears seemed to wrinkle. 'Think, Fupi.'

The others looked from one to another.

'Got it!' cried Lucy, leaping up.

Fupi fell onto the floor with a bump, then jumped up and ran round barking "*Eureka*", or whatever it is dogs say when they've made a great discovery.

'Tell us,' said Mum.

'There's your answer,' cried Lucy, pointing at Fupi.

'I told you it meant soft in the head,' said Kal.

'No, listen. Ellie, tell us again what Matata said.'

'It sounded like: *mahali pa mfupi ya kichwa.*'

'And you said it meant: the Place of the Short of the Head?'

'Something like that.'

'The *mfupi* bit means short. Right?'

'Yes.'

'And Fupi's called *mfupi*, because she's short.'

'*I* told you that,' said Kal.

'All right, but Craig told *you.*'

'Lucy, that's it!' cried Ellie. 'The Place of Fupi's Head. Like that's called *Mlima ya Simba* – Lion Hill.' She pointed to the hill

85

overlooking the house. 'This is a place where there's a rock or hill or something, which is shaped like Fupi's head.'

'Exactly!' cried Lucy. 'Fupi, you are clever, having a place named after you.'

'Well *done*, you two,' said Mum.

Craig shook his head. 'Sorry, guys, that won't wash.'

'Why?' said Kal.

'Remember, Matata never met Fupi before he came to us, and it's almost certain his father didn't. So, there's no way the father would name a place after a dog he'd never met.'

'Oh,' said Lucy, slumping in her seat. 'I thought we'd solved the mystery.'

'I think we *have* solved it, but not quite as you've suggested. I think it's something rather more sinister.'

Mum and Ellie exchanged glances.

'Ellie,' said Craig, 'you said you couldn't be sure you'd heard Matata correctly. Could he have said: *mahali pa mfupa ya kichwa?*'

'What's the difference?' asked Lucy.

'*Mfupi* means short; but *mfupa* means bone.'

'The Place of the Bone of the Head,' said Lucy slowly.

'I think so. And what's that, Lucy?'

This time it came. 'The skull,' she said slowly. 'The Place of the Skull.'

'I guess so.'

'Do you know where it is, Craig,' asked Mum.

'No, I've never heard of it.'

'Ellie, does Matata know?' asked Lucy.

'No. His father told him about the place but never took him there, but I think it's somewhere in those hills where we found him.'

'The Seki Hills?' said Craig. 'Could be.'

'Where we're going tomorrow,' said Mum.

'I'm glad I'm not coming,' said Ellie.

Chapter 15

Disaster

Dad had hardly finished breakfast next morning before he was pacing up and down, looking at his watch and saying things like: 'Long day ahead of us,' and: 'We don't want to leave it too late,' and: 'It can get dark quite quickly in the tropics. Ah, at last.'

Joel drove up in the Land Rover and Dad hurried down the steps and climbed in. Mum, Craig and Kal followed, and Joel drove them down to the airstrip.

Twenty minutes later, they were airborne and Craig flew back and forth over the Seki Hills, while Dad peered out of the window, consulting his GPS, making notes and taking photographs. After a while, he tapped Craig on the shoulder.

'I've seen enough from the air,' he shouted.

Craig nodded and turned towards their new airstrip.

After a rather bumpy landing, they climbed out and sat in the shade of the wing, sipping cold drinks from the cool box which Craig had brought, and watching Dad lay out some aerial photographs on the ground.

'Craig, these are the photos you and Kal took. I was studying them yesterday evening.'

'We're about here,' said Craig.

Dad made a mark. 'How far away are these places? I'd like to start with them.' He pointed at crosses he'd made.

'That one's probably about a mile and a half. The other's a bit further.'

'We should be getting along, then.'

Craig turned to Mum and Kal. 'You guys, okay, or do you want to wait here?'

'It's lovely being the open,' she said. 'I'm coming.'

'Me too,' said Kal.

Craig put the cool box back in the plane, and returned

carrying a rucksack and his rifle. He must have seen Mum's nervous look. 'Just in case, Sarah. We might meet a lion or a buffalo.'

'Or an elephant,' murmured Kal.

***

Two hours later, they finished their survey of the first spot marked on the photograph. Dad had collected several samples, but was clearly not finding anything of interest.

'A bit disappointing,' he said. 'Can we move on?'

'Let's have a break, first.' Craig set down his rifle and rucksack in the shade of a tree.

'What a beautiful spot,' said Mum.

A bang!

Craig cried out.

Mum whirled round.

Craig slumped to the ground.

Dad flung himself down beside him. 'Craig!'

There was a rattle of stones. Three men carrying guns came out of the bush towards them.

***

Kal was stunned. The sound of the shot was still ringing in his ears.

One of the men was tall and Kal could just make out something on his black T-shirt. Rat-Man!

Another scream from Mum.

Kal tore his eyes away.

Craig lay on the ground, blood spreading across his shirt.

Dad was holding him, a look of horror on his face.

Craig didn't move.

Kal turned and ran. He had one thought: get help.

Another shot.

It ricocheted off a rock.

Another.

A spurt of dust leapt up near his feet. He twisted and dodged between two trees. A bullet thudded into one them.

Kal tried to run faster.

Where's the plane? Where is it?

He swerved round a rock and glanced over his shoulder.

Rat-Man was after him. He'd left his rifle, but in his hand was a *simi*, the sun glinting on the blade.

Where's the plane?

The man was gaining on him.

Kal swerved towards some bushes. Thorns tugged at him, scratching his face, ripping his shirt, tearing his legs. He didn't slacken speed.

Rat-Man was behind him, struggling and cursing and hacking at the thorn bushes with his *simi*.

Kal gained a few precious metres and raced clear. His eyes were misting. He wiped his hand across them.

Blood.

He hardly noticed. He darted round a clump of rocks. Then another thicket of bushes.

Round another thicket.

Still no sign of the plane.

What was Rat-Man doing here?

Kal swerved to the left, ran a couple of hundred metres and threw himself down behind a jumble of rocks. His heart was pounding as though it would burst out of his chest and a metal band was tightening round his heart. He was sucking in lungfuls of air, desperately trying to relieve the pain. Gradually, his breathing eased and the band loosened. Blood was streaming from numerous cuts and scratches on his legs and arms.

He felt nothing.

He raised his head. Had he escaped? He listened. No sound of pounding feet. No sound of panting breath. No chink of stones from someone creeping among the rocks.

But there was a sound, a strange sound, a ridiculous sound – as though someone was sawing wood.

The noise was coming from behind him.

He slowly turned his head.

There was a blur of movement.

Kal twisted away just in time.

The snake, its mouth wide open, was so close that its skin

brushed his arm. It wasn't a big snake, but it was thickset with a diamond pattern down its body.

Kal's eyes were wide with terror.

The snake drew back its head.

Kal didn't wait. He hurled himself to the side and leapt up just as the snake struck again, missed, and thumped into the sand.

Kal ran.

He came clear of the rocks. And there ahead of him was the plane.

But it was nearly a mile away.

His eyes caught a flash of sun on a *simi*. Rat-Man was walking slowly studying the ground, following Kal's tracks. As soon as Kal appeared, he gave a shout and set off after him.

Kal could never outrun this man, a man who knew the bush, had lived all his life here. What hope did he have – even if he was a good runner – an eleven-year-old boy against a fully-grown man who hunted in the bush for his livelihood?

Why hadn't he told Reuben about Rat-Man when they were at the hotel? Why, oh why? Now it was too late.

Reuben!

Kal's mind suddenly cleared. His shoulders relaxed and his stride increased. He was no longer in the bush. He was in the Olympic stadium. The noise of the crowd was deafening. The hurdles and the water-jump flowed past. His chest was tightening. He shut out the pain. He forced his shoulders to relax. He had to keep his rhythm. He was coming off the final bend. The finish was ahead. He threw his chest out. His arms began to pump. He dug into reserves he didn't know he had. He flew.

He tore open the door of the plane. Scrambled into the seat.

The keys!

The spare keys! Where does Craig keep the spare ignition keys? He scrabbled in all possible hiding places. The sun visor. Yes!

What do I do?

He turned the ignition switch.

90

Nothing.

Think! Master switch. He tried again. There was a whirring sound.

Think! Fuel primer.

'Come on, come on!'

The engine sprang to life. No time to do the checks.

He opened the throttle. The plane juddered. Kal operated the foot pedals and turned onto the airstrip.

Rat-Man was running towards him.

Kal set his mouth in a thin line, gritted his teeth, increased the revs, raced forward.

The man threw his *simi*. It bounced harmlessly off a wing.

Kal gripped the controls, his whole body tense. He held his line.

Rat-Man hurled himself aside just in time.

The plane swept past, covering him in a cloud of dust.

Kal was away.

Chapter 16

Terrible News

Lucy was helping Joel carry out some repairs to the orphan pens.

Matata came and watched. At first, he was shy but when it came to feeding time, he joined in and helped.

Lucy thought he might be rough with the animals, having been a poacher, but then she saw he had a special way with them.

It was mid-afternoon before they finished, and Lucy was exhausted. 'Phew,' she said, 'that took ages.'

'That was very good, Lucy,' said Joel. 'Go and have some food.'

She ran back to the house for a late lunch, and found Ellie on the veranda reading a book.

'We've kept some lunch for you.' Ellie pointed to some dishes on the sideboard covered with a cloth.

'Great. I'm starving.' Lucy drank two glasses of fruit juice, collected some food, and slumped down in a chair, with Fupi at her feet waiting for scraps. 'When do you think the others will be back?'

Ellie shrugged.

***

Lucy had dozed off but was woken by the sound of a vehicle. She hadn't heard the plane, but that would be Joel coming back with the others. She and Fupi ran out to meet them.

Then she stopped. Joel had only Kal with him. He was getting out of the vehicle. His shirt was torn and he was crying. He never did that – not even the time he broke his arm playing football. And he was covered in blood.

'What is it?' She rushed up to the vehicle. 'Kal, what is it? What's happened? Where are the others?'

'Oh, Lucy! Craig's been shot.'

'What!' Ellie had come down the steps. 'What do you mean?'

'Craig's dead – he's been shot.'

'No!' Ellie screamed. 'And Mum and Dad?'

'They're okay, but... but... Ellie, he wasn't moving.'

'Dead!' wailed Lucy.

The three of them clung to each other sobbing. Fupi ran round them looking puzzled.

'I need to tell Diana,' said Joel, and hurried off.

A few moments later, Diana joined them. All the colour had drained from her face. 'Come inside, children,' she said, in a cracked voice. She led them to the veranda and made them sit down.

Martha came in with mugs of tea and handed them round. She too was crying.

Lucy put her tea down, threw her arms round Martha's neck and sobbed.

Then Diana said quietly: 'Joel has told me a bit, Kal. Can you tell us what happened?'

Lucy looked up but still clung to Martha.

Kal wiped his arm across his eyes. 'I think it was poachers. We were about to have lunch when I saw these men with guns. One of them pointed his gun at us and—' He put his head into his hands. '— there was this shot and Craig fell to the ground and... and there was blood coming from his chest and... Mum was screaming and Dad was holding him and...' He sobbed again. 'And I saw the men coming towards us, so I ran to get help.'

'Where?' said Ellie.

'I ran to the plane and flew back.' He made it sound as though he'd just ridden his bike back from school.

'You're covered in blood,' said Lucy.

'Lucy, Craig wasn't moving,' he whispered.

Samson came running. 'What's happened?' He rushed up to Kal's chair.

'I think they were poachers,' said Kal, and retold the story.

'You did well.' Samson gripped Kal's shoulder. 'Those men, did you recognise them?'

93

'One of them was Rat-Man.'

Ellie didn't laugh this time.

'We saw him at the hotel. I thought him and his mate were going to nick the Range Rover.'

'What hotel? What Range Rover?'

Kal explained. 'He also tried to run down Craig,' he added. 'I'm sure he did.'

'So,' said Samson, 'these men are working for Nagu. You're sure it was the same men?'

'Almost certain.'

Samson stood up and took a mobile phone from his pocket. They watched and waited as he called a number.

Samson tried again. 'It's no good. I can't get a signal. I'll try the radio.' He hurried into Craig's office.

More waiting. No one said anything. They just looked at one another and tried to overhear what Samson was saying.

Finally he emerged. 'Either the police are not answering, or their radio's broken.'

'What can we do?' wailed Lucy, panic rising in her voice. 'What will happen to Craig's... Craig's...? What about Mum and Dad?'

'We can't just leave them,' cried Ellie.

'I'll go out there with some of the men,' said Samson.

'No.' Diana shook her head.

'But we must.'

'You can't go now, Samson. It will soon be dark. There's nothing you or anyone can do until it gets light.'

Samson rubbed his hands over his face. 'You're right, Diana. I'll tell Joel to fetch the cattlemen to spend the night here and we'll leave first thing in the morning.'

***

After supper – which no one felt like eating – they gathered round the table and discussed their plan.

Lucy remembered she and Kal had once watched a war film about some commandoes planning a raid. They had been sitting round a table the night before, just like this. The only difference was, this was for real.

'Kal has to come to show us the way,' said Samson, 'but Lucy and Ellie must stay here.'

'No way,' said Lucy. And she could see Ellie shaking her head.

'Samson's right,' said Diana, dabbing her eyes. 'We cannot risk anyone else getting hurt.'

'But Mum and Dad are somewhere out there,' said Ellie. 'We can't stay here.'

'It's too dangerous,' said Samson.

'We're coming with you,' said Lucy.

Diana shook her head. 'Samson and the others can't be responsible for you.'

'We can look after ourselves,' said Ellie. 'Lucy's right. We have to come.'

Diana sighed. 'What do you think, Samson?'

'I'm not happy.'

'Nor am I.'

'We're coming,' said Ellie quietly.

Lucy glanced at her sister. What a change from the Ellie who had arrived at Simba and thrown a wobbly because Craig suggested she change her shoes before going camping.

Samson and Diana had a whispered conversation.

'All right.' Samson pursed his lips. 'But you stay with me at all times and do exactly as I tell you. Is that understood?'

The girls nodded.

He stood up. 'I'll go and talk to the men.'

As soon as he left, Diana turned to the children. 'You heard what Samson said: early start tomorrow. Off you go now.'

They murmured their goodnights and trooped off the veranda.

Lucy glanced back at Diana, and saw silent tears starting. Poor Diana; Craig was her only son.

Lucy ran and hugged her then went to Ellie's room, sobbing.

There was no way she was going to be on her own tonight.

Chapter 17

Matata Finds the Way

Lucy was alone in the forest. Someone or something was following. It was getting dark. She heard a horrible squeaky laugh. It was Moshi with the face of a toad. She started running. Couldn't see where she was going. Heavy breathing. She didn't know the way. Tried running faster. She tripped and tumbled into a great dark hole. Suddenly, there was Craig. He caught her and she clung to him. 'It's all right, Lucy. Everything's all right.' He was smiling.

She was instantly wide-awake. 'Ellie, Ellie, wake up.' She sat up and shook her sister.

'What is it?'

'Wake up.'

'Leave me alone, I need to sleep.'

'But Ellie – everything's all right.'

Ellie sat up with a start. 'What do you mean?'

'It was Craig – he says everything's all right.'

Ellie put her arms round Lucy. 'It was a dream.'

'I suppose so, but it, it seemed so real.'

Ellie switched on a torch and checked her watch. 'It's only just after two, Lucy. Go back to sleep.'

'Ellie, we don't need to be sad; it's all going to be okay.' She could tell her sister was watching her in the dark. 'The dream was as real as you sitting here.'

'That's scary.'

'Ellie, it's true.'

***

The next thing Lucy knew, Martha had come in with tea. She checked her watch: just after four.

She and Ellie changed into their day things and hurried out to the veranda. It was still dark but Kal and the others were already there.

Martha and Matata were taking round mugs of tea. Three cattlemen, dressed in their Maasai warrior clothes, were sitting on the steps of the veranda, warming their hands on their mugs, but they weren't laughing and joking as they normally did. Just chatting quietly. Their red blankets covered their heads and shoulders to protect against the cool morning air, and their spears were stuck in the ground nearby.

Lucy knew Onesmo, who was one of the men who had brought in Mondo the serval with the spear wound. She particularly liked him because he had taken her several times to see the cows with calves. And he had let her bottle-feed a calf whose mother had been killed by a lion. She recognised the other two, but couldn't remember their names.

Diana was talking to Samson and Joel, while Kal sat hunched in a chair sipping his tea and gazing into the darkness. Lucy longed to tell him everything was going to be all right but she wasn't sure he'd understand.

'*Tuende* – let's go.' Samson got to his feet.

'Just a minute,' said Diana. She went into the office and returned with a rifle. 'You may need this.'

Samson held her eyes briefly. 'I've got the radio in the Land Rover. We'll keep in touch.'

Diana hugged the children. 'Come back safely. All of you,' she whispered, then turned away and wiped her eyes.

***

Samson drove, with Matata and Kal beside him. Lucy and Ellie sat on the middle seat with Fupi between them. Joel and the three cattlemen sat behind.

No one spoke.

It was the first time the children had been driving in the bush in the dark. Lucy wished things weren't so tense so they could stop and study the night animals glimpsed in the headlights: nightjars swooping to catch moths caught in the beam of the lights, a honey-badger bumbling off home, loads of spring hares bouncing around like miniature kangaroos, and even a snuffly old aardvark. But today, game viewing was the last thing they were thinking about.

There was a crackle on the two-way radio and Diana's voice came through the darkness. 'How is it Samson? Over.'

'No problem. We expect to be at the place in about two hours. Over.'

'Good, let me speak to Kal. Over.'

Samson passed the radio across.

'Kal, do you think you can find the place? Over.'

'Yes, Joel and I know where it is. Over.'

Lucy was sure Kal had often imagined himself going off on an early morning raid like those commandoes in the film, and communicating in radio-speak with base, but he could never have imagined anything like this.

'Good luck. Keep in touch. Over and out.'

'Over and out.' Kal passed the radio back to Samson and continued to stare ahead.

It seemed almost no time before the sun came over the horizon. Samson turned off the headlights. The day quickly warmed up and they took off their sweaters and threw them into the back.

The hills came gradually nearer and Lucy began to worry. Had she really seen Craig? Was everything really going to be all right?

Samson and Kal were talking in low voices. Kal seemed to know exactly where to go. Lucy felt very proud of her brother – but she would never tell him that.

They arrived at the edge of the hills, and Kal pointed upwards. It was now very rough but the Land Rover kept moving forward like some willing workhorse ploughing through sand, scrabbling over rocks and flattening bushes in its relentless climb.

They finally reached a plateau which Lucy recognised. 'This is where we came before. Where you made the airstrip.'

'Yeah,' said Kal. 'When we came here yesterday we started from over there by those trees.'

Samson drove across, and they climbed out and stretched their cramped limbs. Fupi started sniffing around, and Joel and Matata began searching for tracks.

'*Nyayo hapa*,' called Matata. The men gathered round him and peered at the ground.

'What is it, Ellie?' asked Lucy.

'Matata's found some footprints.'

Samson spoke briefly to Joel and Matata. They went to the back of the vehicle and Joel returned with his spear, and Matata with his bow and arrows – he must have found where Craig had hidden them.

'Kal,' said Samson, 'can you describe the place where it all happened?'

'Sure.' Kal picked up a stick, and everyone squatted down on their haunches and watched him draw a map in the sand with Joel adding some details. There was much nodding and *eehing*.

When Kal had finished, Joel and Matata stood up and shook everyone by the hand. Without another word, they crossed over a gully and went loping off, as effortlessly as gazelles – Matata's leg being now almost healed.

In a few minutes they were out of sight.

'Good luck,' whispered Lucy.

'What do we do now, Samson?' asked Kal.

'We wait.'

Ellie went to the vehicle and came back with a tin of biscuits and some bananas. The cattlemen made a fire, and soon they were sitting in the shade nibbling the food and sipping tea, but no one talked.

'Should we call Diana?' asked Ellie.

'I'll do that.' Kal jumped to his feet. 'What shall I say?'

'Tell her we've arrived at the airstrip,' said Samson, 'and that Joel and Matata have gone to find the place. The rest of us are waiting.'

Lucy ate another banana and gave Fupi a biscuit.

Kal returned after a few minutes. 'Diana says good luck.' He took a banana and sat down on his own, his back against a tree, and gazed into space.

There was nothing to do but wait.

It seemed to Lucy they had been there for hours, when Fupi pricked her ears and growled.

The men, whom Lucy thought had gone to sleep, sat up instantly – their hands on their spears – but they relaxed when they saw a grinning Joel come loping into view, followed by Matata.

Fupi ran over to them, sniffed them, wagged her tail, and being satisfied went and lay down in the shade of the vehicle.

'We found the place,' called Joel. 'And we found this.' He held up a small brass tube.

There were sharp intakes of breath from the cattlemen, and exclamations of '*aieeh*!'

'What is it?' said Lucy.

'Can I see?' said Kal.

Joel passed it to him.

'Probably a three-o-three,' said Kal in a flat voice.

'A what?' said Ellie.

'Cartridge from the bullet which killed Craig.' Kal was on the verge of tears again.

'But Craig is not dead!' cried Joel. 'I think he is hurt but he can walk.'

'What!'

'*Kwele* – true. That one, he is strong like a buffalo – *kama nyati*.'

The cattlemen nodded and said '*eeh*'; then chattered away, huge grins on their faces.

'I knew it,' said Lucy. 'I said everything was going to be all right.'

Kal looked puzzled.

'Did you see anyone?' asked Samson.

'No,' said Joel, 'but Matata found the way they went.'

'How many people?'

'Many.'

'That's Mum, Dad, Craig and the men who attacked us?' said Kal, his face now shining.

'We think,' said Joel. 'Those men, their tracks are the ones we saw the other day.'

'I'll call Diana,' said Samson.

When he returned, he gathered everyone together. 'Diana

was very pleased.' He looked round the group. 'Are we all ready, now? *Tayari?*'

There were nods all round.

'Lucy, will you and Ellie be all right?'

'Yes.' Lucy glanced at the men hardened by life in the bush, and wondered if she and Ellie really would. She gritted her teeth and caught Ellie's eye. Ellie nodded. They jolly well would be all right.

Samson looked doubtful, but all he said was: 'We have to move quickly and quietly.' He packed his rucksack with water and some food, collected the rifle and locked the Land Rover.

They set off across the gully, following Joel and Matata.

Lucy tried not to imagine too much, and not to think how hot it was, and how thirsty and weary she felt. *And* whether they might walk straight into an ambush and be shot.

They had been walking for ages, when Joel stopped them and pointed to a patch of ground. 'This is where Craig fell.'

Lucy peered, blinked and rubbed her eyes. How on earth can Joel make sense of a few scuff-marks on the ground?

Matata indicated a dark bit on the sand. '*Damu.*'

'What's that, Ellie?' whispered Lucy.

'Blood'

Although it was baking hot, Lucy couldn't help shivering. They had walked half-way across Africa and found a tiny patch of dark sand, and... and it was Craig's blood. Life in England had never prepared her for anything like this.

'*Hapa na hapa,*' said Matata, pointing at other places.

'He says, here and here,' whispered Ellie, 'but I can't see anything.'

'Nor can I,' said Lucy.

'See here,' said Joel. 'Craig is now standing again.'

Lucy had given up trying to read anything into the marks on the ground, and simply accepted what Joel was saying.

Joel, Matata and the cattlemen began scrutinising the ground and their surroundings, calling to each other and pointing out things. There was a shout from Onesmo, who was digging in a tree with his spear. A few minutes later he came over to

Samson holding something in his hand. '*Risasi*.'

'What is it, Samson?' asked Lucy.

'A bullet.'

'In the tree? How did it get there?'

Samson shrugged.

'Kal, do you know?' asked Lucy.

Kal had gone very pale. He took the bullet from Samson. 'No.'

'*Hapa*,' called Matata.

'This is the way,' said Samson.

Lucy noticed Kal slip the bullet into his pocket.

'Is it much further?' asked Ellie, wiping her hand across her forehead. Her face was looking red.

'I don't know,' said Samson. 'Are you all right?'

'Yes,' she said fiercely.

But Lucy could see she was struggling. *She* was, as well, but she knew they couldn't let these brilliant people down by being wimps.

'Have a drink,' said Samson, passing her a water bottle.

'Thanks,' said Ellie. 'We should go on now.'

Lucy couldn't understand how Joel and Matata could possibly see where to go, but every now and then, one would point out something on the ground: a broken twig, a speck of blood, a disturbed rock, a crushed blade of grass. The other would nod, and they would hurry on.

Eventually, they came to an open area where a small stream ran across bare rocks and disappeared over a ledge into a pool below. They stopped and splashed cool water over their faces and arms then crossed to the shade of a tree and ate the remaining bananas.

Fupi went off to explore, and Kal took off his trainers and socks to paddle in the shallow stream. 'Come on, guys.'

'Is it all right, Samson?' asked Lucy. She'd been told by Ellie about some nasty disease you could get in Africa by paddling.

'No problem, but be careful. It's very slippery.'

Ellie and Lucy joined Kal, and they splashed and slipped and slithered in the cool water, and for a moment forgot their worries and fears. Then they sat on the warm rocks letting the sun dry their legs.

Lucy studied the massive rocky hillside which rose up in front of them. Although she was worrying about what lay ahead, she couldn't help gazing in awe at the scenery.

What a beautiful country, she thought, and that rock face is amazing.

Higher up, were what appeared to be caves.

'I wonder if anything lives in those caves,' she said.

'Craig says leopards live in caves,' said Kal.

'And bats,' added Lucy.

'I don't like bats,' said Ellie, 'they get in your hair.'

'That's rubbish!'

'No, it's—'

'*Aieeh!*'

The children spun round to see Matata yelling and pointing.

Chapter 18

The Place of the Skull

Everyone stared at Matata.

'*Mahali pa mfupa ya kichwa*,' he screeched, pointing at the rock face.

'What is it?' whispered Lucy.

'He says, it's the Place of the Skull,' said Ellie, in a strangled voice.

'Yes,' cried Kal. 'Look! Those caves we were looking at. There, see! Those could be two eyes, and the one below could be a mouth.'

'And that jagged bit in the middle could be the nose,' cried Lucy.

A cloud drifted across the sun, and suddenly it felt much cooler.

'I don't like this,' said Ellie.

Matata's eyes were wide with fear and he was trembling. Samson put a firm arm round his shoulders, but it took several minutes before he settled.

'It is the place, Samson, isn't it?' said Lucy.

'I think so.'

The rock face, which earlier had seemed so majestic, now appeared sinister and menacing. Vultures were soaring in the air currents rising above it.

A sudden bark distracted them. Fupi was upstream and was sniffing at something on the ground, her tail wagging madly.

'Let's go and see.' Kal jumped up and ran across the rocks in his bare feet.

Lucy and Ellie followed.

'What is it?' called Lucy.

Fupi looked up. Her tongue was hanging out and she seemed to be grinning.

'What is—? It's a hankie.' Lucy picked it up. 'There are some

104

initials here in the— It's Mum's!'

They raced back to show the others.

'Well done,' cried Samson. 'So we know they were here.'

'But where did they go?' said Ellie.

'Come and see what Joel found.' Samson led them across the rocks to where even Lucy could make out the remains of a fire.

Joel put his hand to it. 'It is still warm. I think they left about four hours ago.'

'So they spent the night here?' said Lucy.

'Yes.'

'Come on,' said Samson. 'Time to go.'

The children gathered up their socks and trainers, and as Lucy began to put on hers, she noticed a piece of greenish rock by her foot. She glanced round to check the others weren't watching then picked it up and studied it. There was a hint of red in it, but this wasn't brownish red like the other stones she'd found; this was bluish red. And *there* was another piece. And another. She quickly slipped them into the pocket of her shorts without saying anything. She wasn't going to risk making a fool of herself again. She finished tying her laces, scrambled to her feet and hurried to catch up with the others.

After a while, the trail began to head downwards. They rounded the side of a hill and there was the plain below them, but the hillside was rough with thorny bushes and spiky trees. It would take quite a while to reach the plain.

They continued downwards, and every so often, Matata would kneel to inspect the invisible trail or pick up a pinch of dust and let it float away to test the direction of the wind.

They were about half way down when Joel held up his hand. He turned his head and listened.

'What is it?' Lucy whispered.

'Sh!' Samson unslung his rifle.

Lucy couldn't hear a thing – only birds.

Joel pointed with his *simi*.

Samson lined up the rifle.

Lucy thought she heard a *tssk, tssk* sound and then some

birds, about the size of starlings, flew up.

Joel put his finger to his lips and signalled them to move back.

Lucy glanced nervously at him. 'What is—?'

'Run!'

Joel grabbed Lucy's arm and pulled her after him.

Onesmo seized Ellie and almost carried her.

Samson remained motionless, his rifle aimed straight ahead.

Kal and the others were already running.

There was a snort and crashing through the bushes near where they had been standing.

Lucy glimpsed an enormous black shape careering down the hill.

Buffalo! They had nearly walked into a buffalo.

Joel stopped and let go of Lucy's arm. He was laughing.

'Joel!' cried Ellie. 'Someone could have been killed.'

He shrugged. '*Labda* – perhaps.' He was still laughing.

'And you can laugh?'

'No one *was* killed.'

'Honestly!'

'How did you know the buffalo was there?' asked Lucy, still panting. 'I didn't see a thing.'

'The birds,' said Joel.

'Birds? What birds?'

'Oxpeckers – tick birds,' said Samson, joining them and unloading the rifle. 'They feed on ticks and things which live on the buffaloes and act as watchmen.'

'*Macho ya nyati*,' said Matata.

'What's that mean?' asked Lucy.

'The eyes of the buffalo,' said Samson. 'The birds have very good eyes and warn the buffaloes if anything is coming.'

'*Namna hii*,' said Matata, and gave the *tssk, tssk* sound which Lucy had heard.

'The wind changed,' said Joel, 'and he caught our smell.'

'Kal's feet, probably,' said Lucy.

'Hey, watch it!'

'Are we safe yet?' asked Ellie, as the colour began to return to her cheeks.

'He is now far,' said Joel. 'He was frightened.'

'*He* was frightened!'

'It was a male on his own,' said Samson. 'Those ones can be bad. Very bad.'

'It says in my book that more people in Africa are killed by buffaloes than by any other wild animal,' said Lucy.

'*Kwele* – true,' said Joel.

'Great!' said Ellie. 'You've just made my day.'

'At least, it's another bird for the list,' said Lucy.

'Poxy birds,' muttered Kal.

'You can say that,' said Lucy, 'but if it hadn't been for them we could have walked right into that buffalo.'

'Ner. I'd seen it and was about to warn you all.'

'Yeah, right. Like we believe you.'

Samson handed round the water bottle; then they resumed their journey and reached the plain without further excitement.

Lucy was relieved because she could now empty all the grit out of her trainers.

Joel pointed at the sand. 'Those ones have been picked by a vehicle.'

There was no mistaking the signs this time. Even Lucy could see the tyre tracks.

Matata, who was moving round and peering at the ground, gave a shout.

They hurried over to where he was pointing at a game trail going off in the opposite direction to the tyre tracks.

'What is it, Matata?' asked Lucy.

Ellie translated for her. 'He says some people have gone away on foot but others have gone in the vehicle.'

'Who?'

'Come off it, Lucy,' said Ellie. 'Even Joel and Matata can't tell that just by looking at footprints.'

'I think your Mum, Dad and Craig went in the vehicle,' said Samson. 'Probably someone came to meet them.'

He turned and had a quick discussion with Joel and Onesmo, who then ran off.

'Where are they going?' asked Lucy.

'To get our Land Rover,' said Samson. 'We'll wait here in the shade.'

'Where did that other vehicle go, Samson?' asked Ellie, as they settled under the trees. 'The one with Mum, Dad and Craig.'

'Joel thinks, there.' Samson pointed.

Matata hissed, and Lucy's fear returned.

She could just make out a rundown *manyatta* in the distance.

Chapter 19

Ellie's Scary Plan

It was almost dark by the time Joel and Onesmo returned with the Land Rover. There was a brief discussion, and Lucy could see Onesmo and the two cattlemen nodding and looking excited, but there was also a hard look in their eyes.

'What's happening?' she whispered to Ellie.

'They're going hunting.'

'What for?'

'Don't be thick, Lucy,' said Kal.

'Those men?'

'The ones who went that way.' Samson pointed to the game trail Matata had discovered.

'*Tuende* – let's go,' said Onesmo. The men grasped their spears and ran off down the path.

As Lucy watched them go, their bounding steps reminded her of Joel and Matata, and of the Maasai she and Kal had seen on TV running in the London marathon.

The rest of them climbed into the Land Rover and they set off, Samson driving.

It wasn't long before he had difficulty seeing the track, but it wouldn't be safe to turn on the vehicle's lights, so Joel and Matata got out and ran ahead to show the way.

Very soon, the moon rose bathing everywhere in ghostly light which helped Samson see the track.

They had been driving for about twenty minutes when Joel and Matata stopped and came up to Samson's window.

'We are now close to that *manyatta*,' said Joel. 'Matata will go and see.'

'Shouldn't you go with him?' said Ellie.

'No, the dogs there know Matata. They won't worry if they smell him, but if I go they may give the alarm.'

Samson beckoned to Matata and whispered instructions to

him. Matata grinned but Samson looked worried as his new son disappeared into the darkness.

The rest of them climbed out of the vehicle and waited.

This was the worst of all the waits that day. Lucy couldn't help worrying about Matata, about Onesmo and the two cattlemen, and she felt sick with worry about Mum, Dad and Craig.

A deep "*hoo hoo*" came from the darkness.

Ellie whimpered, and although Lucy knew it was only an owl, she couldn't stop the sudden shiver.

Another eerie hoot.

Lucy wondered if it was a sign of terrible disaster to come. She peered at the tree where the sound was coming from and could just make out the silhouette of a massive eagle owl in the bright moonlight.

There was a hiss from nearby and Lucy started.

Fupi growled.

Matata appeared out of the night and spoke to Samson.

Ellie translated for Kal and Lucy. 'Mum, Dad and Craig *are* there,' she whispered.

Lucy gave a gasp of excitement.

'They've been put in a hut, and there are two men outside guarding with spears. Matata overheard them talking. It was someone the men called the Big Man who picked up Mum, Dad and Craig in the hills.'

'The Big Man – who's he?'

'Matata's not sure,' said Ellie, 'but he thinks it could be the one Kal calls Toad-Face.'

'Toad-Face!'

'Sh – yes, and he may come back tonight to get them.'

'What's Toad-Face going to do?'

'Matata doesn't know.'

Samson then started a whispered discussion with Joel. Samson seemed to suggest one thing and Joel another, which Samson clearly disagreed with.

'What's happening, Ellie?' whispered Lucy, but Ellie was too intent on listening. Then she butted in. Samson and Joel seemed surprised to be interrupted, but they listened. Then they nodded. Then they smiled and shook Ellie's hand.

When she explained her plan to Kal and Lucy, *they* didn't smile. The plan was brilliant, but really scary.

They all scrambled back into the Land Rover.

Samson started the engine, turned the headlights full on and set off.

There was no going back now.

The moon disappeared behind a bank of cloud.

***

Ellie had her eyes tightly shut. Me and my big mouth. What have I let myself in for? I could really screw up. Then, where will we be? And what'll happen to Mum, Dad and Craig?

Samson stopped the Land Rover.

Ellie opened her eyes.

The engine was still running and the headlights were on full-beam illuminating the *manyatta* which appeared even more sinister and rundown in the glare. Two men with spears stood guard outside one of the huts, trying to shield their eyes.

'Go,' whispered Samson.

Ellie felt Lucy give her hand a squeeze. Her mouth was dry. She'd forgotten her Swahili. It wouldn't work.

'Go,' repeated Samson.

It *would* work.

It *had to* work.

Ellie tried to shut out all the what-ifs and slipped out of the vehicle, being careful to keep in the dark behind the lights.

She called out.

The guards were staring straight at her and didn't move. They must be able to see her. Her stomach knotted. She called out louder. The men whispered to each other. Ellie kept talking – now more insistent. One of them went into a hut, and emerged with ole-Tisip. Ellie's heart missed a beat. He was wearing a black T-shirt with a rat on it. Kal *was* right.

Ole-Tisip, Rat-Man – whatever he was called – looked furious as he brandished his club. She remembered it was called a *rungu*. What a time to remember that!

111

He waved his hands at the blinding lights and shouted.

Ellie kept talking.

One of the guards went inside the hut.

Then, *Mum, Dad and Craig emerged.* They stood blinking in the light, looking fearfully at Rat-Man waving his *rungu*.

Craig was holding his arm across his chest and his shirt was covered in blood. Ellie's heart jolted, but she kept talking.

The guards prodded Mum, Dad and Craig towards the light with their spears.

Craig shouted something about turning out that confounded light, and Dad was complaining about something else. Mum seemed bewildered.

The three of them stumbled forward. As soon as they came clear of the lights, Kal, Joel and Matata grabbed them and bundled them into the Land Rover.

Ellie shouted to Rat-Man then ran to the back of the vehicle.

Joel seized her, almost threw her in, and leapt in beside her.

Samson shot backwards in reverse, slammed the vehicle into first gear and sped off, leaving the *manyatta* enveloped in dust.

'Did you see who that was?' yelled Kal.

***

Samson drove as fast as he dared along the sandy track, but it was several minutes before anyone spoke.

'That was Rat-Man,' whispered Kal. 'He *is* real.'

'That one is very bad,' said Joel from the back.

'He certainly is,' said Craig. 'Well done, you guys. That was awesome – is that right, Kal?'

'Awesome *kabisa*!' cried Matata.

Everyone laughed and the tension began to ease.

'Craig, your shirt's covered in blood,' cried Lucy.

'Probably looks worse than it is.'

'When, when you…' said Kal. 'I thought you'd been—'

'Mum's fainted!' cried Lucy.

'I can't stop,' said Samson, concentrating on the driving. He passed Lucy a water bottle. 'Use this.'

Lucy slopped water on Mum's face. 'Mum, Mum, are you okay?'

'Don't drown her,' cried Kal.

'*You* try sprinkling water while we're bumping along in the dark.'

Mum spluttered, shook her head and sat up. 'Where am I?'

Lucy handed Mum the bottle and she drank the remainder in one go. 'You're with us, Mum. You're all right.'

Mum shook her head and pushed her wet hair off her face. 'What happened?'

'We're the rescue party,' said Kal.

Mum burst into tears.

'Here, Mum.' Lucy put her arm round Mum's shoulder and gave her a hankie. 'You're safe now.'

'Thank you, darling.'

'We found your hankie, Mum.'

'This is mine? The one I left near the place where we spent the night?'

'Yes, Fupi found it.'

'But what were... how did you...?'

'Wasn't Ellie fantastic?' said Kal.

'Where *is* Ellie?'

'I'm here, Mum. Are you okay?'

Mum turned round. 'I'm so relieved to be away from that dreadful place. But how did you know we were there? And where's Mr Nagu?'

'Tell Mum,' said Lucy.

'I'm here, Mrs Bartlett,' came the squeaky voice from the back. 'I trust you enjoyed your stay at my friend's house.'

It was Ellie!

'I hope you were not inconvenienced, Mrs Bartlett.'

'Ellie! You were imitating him?'

'I was so scared.'

'Hey, man, that was incredible,' cried Craig, 'I was completely fooled.'

'So was I,' said Dad. 'Well done, all of you.'

'Have you changed your mind about Toad-Face now, Dad?' asked Kal.

'Yes, I have to admit I misjudged him; not someone to trust.'

The children all began talking at once, describing how Kal had raised the alarm, how they had called the cattlemen together, how they had travelled out in the vehicle, and how they discovered where Mum, Dad and Craig were imprisoned.

'And guess what?' cried Lucy. 'We found the Place of the Skull.'

'What?' exclaimed Craig and Dad together.

'It's got to be the place,' said Kal. 'There's this rock face like with caves and things in it which look like eyes and a mouth.'

'It's really spooky,' said Lucy.

'Where is it?' asked Craig.

'It's that place where we found Mum's hankie,' said Kal.

Lucy wondered. Should I tell them? 'Can I say something?'

'What, darling?' said Mum.

'I think I found some rubies there.'

'Not again,' groaned Kal.

Lucy ignored him. 'These ones look different; not like those barnetts we—'

'Garnets,' said Dad.

'Whatever. Can you look, Dad, when we get back?' She fished the stones out of her pocket and passed them to him.

Samson eased off the accelerator, letting the Land Rover find its way home. The moon emerged from behind the clouds, giving a magical glow to the African night. They drove in contented silence. Everyone relaxed. They would soon be home.

Samson began humming a tune.

'What's that light?' asked Ellie.

'Where?' said Lucy.

'There, behind us.'

Kal turned in his seat. 'We're being followed. Go, Samson!'

Samson floored the accelerator and the fear came flooding back.

Chapter 20

Buffaloes

'Who is it?' asked Lucy, in a shaky voice.

'Nagu,' said Samson, without taking his eyes off the track.

'Toad-Face?'

'I don't like this,' said Craig. 'There's no knowing who he might have with him.'

'Go faster, Samson,' urged Ellie.

The vehicle sped along the rough track. Every time it hit a bump, Craig gasped with pain.

'He's getting closer,' said Kal.

They raced through some trees, the ghostly trunks flashing past and disappearing into the darkness. Almost immediately, the track branched three ways.

'Go left,' shouted Craig, 'and turn your lights off. We may fool him.'

Samson switched off the lights. Despite the bright moonlight, it was hard to see and he had to slow down.

Lucy looked over her shoulder. 'I think he's stopped. I think it's going to work. Yes! He's gone down one of the other tracks.'

'It's not worked,' said Kal. 'He's turning round. If that's Toad-Face in his Range Rover there's no way we can beat him.'

'It's still a good two miles before we get onto the ranch,' said Craig.

'What if he catches us?' cried Mum.

'Let's not find out,' said Craig. 'We'll try and lose him. Joel, you know this area, where can we go?'

Before Joel could reply, Samson swore and slammed on the brakes.

'What is it?' cried Lucy.

'There!'

Lucy gasped.

Buffaloes!

They'd driven into the middle of a herd of buffaloes. Large dark shapes surrounded the vehicle, their eyes reflecting the moonlight.

Everyone in the vehicle held their breath.

Lucy heard the animals snorting. There was a jolt, as one brushed against the vehicle. Then another.

'We're probably all right as long as we don't alarm them,' said Craig.

'Don't alarm them, Samson,' whispered Ellie.

Samson edged forward, still with his lights off.

One or two buffaloes tossed their heads, and shook their great horns. If any of them attacked the vehicle, the metalwork would offer little protection to those inside.

Lucy shrank closer to Mum.

'Toad-Face is right behind, now,' said Kal.

'He's trying to force his way through,' said Dad.

'Idiot,' muttered Craig.

Everyone in the Land Rover heard it: a bellow followed by a great crunch. One of the lights on the vehicle behind went out. Another crunch and another. The other light went out.

'They're sorting him out big time!' yelled Kal.

'He'll be killed!' screamed Lucy.

'He's all right,' called Joel from the back of the Land Rover. 'Those buffaloes are going.'

'So are we,' shouted Samson. He flicked on the lights and sped off.

Nothing was following now.

***

It was almost midnight when they got back to the house. Diana and Martha hurried out to greet them. There were hugs all round and more tears.

As soon as Craig was settled on the sofa, all the different stories had to be retold.

Lucy peered at his wound while Diana dressed it. She'd never seen anyone wounded with bullets like that, but she thought Diana might have done. She seemed to know exactly how to deal with it.

'We need to get you to hospital,' said Diana.

'Mother, don't fuss,' said Craig. 'I just need to rest.'

'Nonsense. It's a deep wound and could turn septic. You're going to Nairobi first thing tomorrow and that's that.'

'Nairobi?' said Lucy.

'Yes,' said Diana. 'I know it's in Kenya, but the local hospitals here probably won't have the necessary facilities.'

'I can't fly with my arm like this,' said Craig.

'I'll fly you,' said Kal.

'You most certainly will not,' said Diana. 'Flying round the ranch is one thing – and what you did was marvellous – but flying to Nairobi is quite different. Craig's licence would be cancelled immediately and he would never be issued with another.'

'We could say it was an emergency,' said Kal.

'I know you only want to help, Kal,' said Diana, 'but one adventure is quite enough. We're taking no more risks. Samson will drive him there first thing tomorrow.'

Lucy sat down beside Craig. 'You *are* going to be all right?'

'Hey, man, what's this?'

'I'm sorry, Craig,' she sniffled, 'I don't want anything to happen to you.'

'Here.' He dug into his pocket and pulled out his hankie.

'Thanks.' She wiped her tears and blew her nose. 'Sorry.'

Kal came and sat on Craig's other side.

'Wasn't Kal brilliant?' said Lucy.

'Not bad.' Craig turned and winked at Kal. 'Man, that was quite something – flying the plane back, hey?'

'I'm not sure what was worst,' said Kal, 'the flying, being chased by Rat-Man, or nearly being bitten by the snake.'

'Snake?' said Lucy. 'You never told us about a snake.'

'I probably forgot.'

'You don't forget about something like *that*.'

'All right, but I had other things to think about.' Kal described the incident.

Craig slowly shook his head. 'Man, you are so lucky – that

117

joker is about the worst we have.'

Kal turned pale. 'What was it?'

'Saw-scaled viper; one of the deadliest snakes in Africa – in the world. Gets its name from the noise it makes rubbing its scales together when it's angry.'

'Huh.' Kal fingered the bullet in his pocket. Better not tell them about that, he thought.

'Craig, what happened to you, Mum and Dad after Kal escaped?' asked Lucy.

'It's all a bit of a blur.' Craig winced as he tried to remember. 'I guess I didn't really come round until I was in Nagu's vehicle. At first, we thought he'd come to rescue us, but as soon as ole-Tisip locked us up, we realised otherwise.'

'He was the one who tried to run you down in Arusha,' said Kal. 'I'm sure it was.'

'So it wasn't an accident?'

'No way! I didn't realise Rat-Man and ole-Tisip were the same guy until I saw him again in that T-shirt this evening.'

'I'm afraid I wasn't in a fit state to notice what he was wearing,' said Craig.

'He's bad news.'

'He certainly is but your mum and dad were brilliant, making sure I had water, dressing my wound and keeping ole-Tisip off—'

'Well, well,' came a voice from the far end of the veranda. Dad was beaming, the light from the microscope reflected on his face.

'What?' called Lucy.

'Lucy, I think you're right this time.'

'How do you mean?'

'I need to get confirmation, but I think the stones you collected from that place, the… what was it?'

'Place of the Skull?'

'Indeed. They appear to me to contain some excellent samples of ruby.'

Lucy didn't remember much after that, except everyone talking at once.

Chapter 21

The Hunters Return

Lucy woke next morning to the sound of voices. She got up and peered out of the window. It was just getting light. Onesmo and the two cattlemen were sitting on the veranda steps, their blankets round their shoulders, and their spears stuck into the ground nearby. They'd walked all the way back through the bush – in the dark!

She dressed and hurried outside.

'*Jambo*,' she called. 'What happened?'

'*Jambo, jambo sana*,' they replied, grinning.

'Was everything all right – *nzuri*?'

'*Nzuri, nzuri*,' they chorused.

She and the men grinned at each other. 'So it really was *nzuri*?'

'*Nzuri, nzuri*,' they repeated.

They tried telling her something, but she couldn't understand what they were saying.

Then Lucy remembered another word. 'Would you like some *chai* – tea, *chai*?'

'*Ndiyo, ndiyo. Nzuri, nzuri*.' By saying every word twice, they probably thought it would help her to understand.

She hurried through to the kitchen.

Martha was setting out mugs, and the kettle was nearly boiling.

'*Jambo*, Martha.'

'*Jambo*, Lucy, *habari ya asubuhi*?'

'What does that mean?'

'How are you this morning?'

'*Nzuri, nzuri*.'

Martha clapped her hands.

Ellie came into the kitchen. 'The cattlemen are back.'

'I know. I was talking to them,' said Lucy. 'At least trying to.'

She and Ellie carried the tea out.

The men made room on the veranda steps and Ellie began chatting to them. There seemed to be a lot more *nzuri-ing* and some *eehing*, and plenty of nodding.

Fupi came and joined Lucy.

'Ellie, what are they saying?'

'I'm finding out how they are.'

'Is that all?'

'It's very rude to ask direct questions.'

'Did they find the men?'

'Lucy!'

'Sorry.'

Finally, Ellie turned to Lucy. 'Lucy, they *did* find the men; they'd lit themselves a fire and the smell of the smoke gave them away. Onesmo and the other two waited until they were asleep then crept up, removed their guns and fired them off.'

'Brilliant!'

'They say the men were so frightened they won't stop running until they get to Kenya.'

The cattlemen, who were laughing at what Ellie was saying, didn't look at all scary now, but Lucy remembered the look of determination in their eyes when they'd set off.

Still laughing, Onesmo lay down on the ground and pretended to be asleep. The other two men made banging noises and Onesmo jumped up, leapt around, then started running in circles and shouting.

Fupi barked.

The others held their sides with laughter.

'What's all this *kelele* about?' Craig appeared, looking tired but much better than last night.

Lucy noticed some blood had seeped through his bandage. 'How are you?' she asked.

'Better now, thanks to a good night's sleep.'

Ellie fetched him a mug of tea.

He said something to the men then joined them on the steps.

The men looked serious for a moment then one of them gave a repeat performance, with Craig joining in the laughter.

Kal arrived looking bleary-eyed. 'Aren't these the guys who went after those men?'

Craig explained.

'Do you think they'll come back?'

'No ways. They're probably thinking they're lucky to be alive.'

'What about the guns?'

Onesmo got up and disappeared round the side of the building, returning a few moments later carrying three guns.

'My rifle!' cried Craig, 'I didn't expect to see that again.' He carefully checked it over.

'What'll happen to the other guns?' asked Lucy.

'I'll hand them over to the police.'

The sun was now well up, and Martha was busy setting the breakfast table. Ellie went to help her.

After shaking hands with everyone, the cattlemen left.

Kal and Lucy stayed sitting either side of Craig, as they watched the sun rise and light up the ranch. Soon the superb starlings were back chattering and searching for breakfast on the lawn.

Lucy glanced at Craig and smiled. It was going to be a beautiful day.

***

Samson brought his Land Rover round as soon as they'd finished breakfast, and Lucy was surprised to see Dad was also ready to leave.

'Must strike while the iron's hot,' he said. 'I'd like to get confirmation on those samples, and Craig has kindly agreed I travel with him to Nairobi. I'm pretty sure I'm right, but my knowledge in some areas is less than—'

'It looks as though everyone's ready,' said Mum, smiling brightly.

'Ah, yes, righty oh. Goodbye, then.'

Dad picked up his bag and went down the veranda steps to the vehicle. 'See you soon.' He climbed in then put his head out of the window. 'This is most exciting. I hope I can come back with good news.'

'Bye, Dad,' chorused the children.

They all trooped down to the vehicle.

Kal carried Craig's bag and loaded it into the back then they all stood around wondering what to say.

'Come back soon,' said Lucy, and sniffed a bit.

He smiled. 'Take care, Lucy.'

Everyone said goodbye, and Craig climbed in.

The children watched and waved until they could no longer see the vehicle's dust cloud. Then Ellie fetched a book. Kal and Matata went to play football. Lucy collected her diary and a blanket, lay down in the shade of a tree with Fupi and fell asleep.

Chapter 22

Kiboko River

Diana had a message on the radio from Samson early next morning, to say that Craig had been treated at the hospital for a chipped collarbone and a deep flesh wound from which a bullet had been removed.

'He's extremely lucky,' said Diana. 'It could have been so much worse.'

Lucy shuddered and tried not to think about it. 'When will he be back?'

'I don't know, dear, the hospital wants to keep him under observation for the next few days, but one thing is certain, Craig will want to get back as soon as possible. He hates cities.'

'Any news from Dad?' asked Ellie.

'Only that Samson is taking him to the geology department in the university today to meet a Professor Wafula.'

'He'll enjoy that,' said Kal. 'Dad likes meeting important people.'

'Mum, do you think Dad was right about those stones?' asked Lucy. 'About them containing rubies and sapphires and things?'

'I do hope so. You know how careful he is about his work.'

'But he could be wrong?'

'Lucy, there's no sense in speculating about what might or might not be, let's wait until he gets back.'

Lucy glanced at Ellie and Kal. She could tell they also were worrying about what might happen to Simba Ranch if Dad was wrong and Craig couldn't get extra money to run it.

Three days later, Diana announced that Craig, Dad and Samson would be leaving Nairobi the next day.

'It's at least an eight-hour drive,' she said. 'They won't be here before mid-afternoon at the earliest. Why don't you children go with Joel and Matata, take a picnic and meet them

123

at the Kiboko River. It's a lovely spot. Joel knows it.'

***

Next day, they arrived at the Kiboko River, climbed out of the Land Rover and surveyed a wide expanse of dry sand.

'This isn't a river,' said Lucy. 'Where's all the water?'

'Come, I will show you,' said Joel.

Kal parked the Land Rover in the shade of a large thorn tree. A pair of brown parrots – another for Lucy's bird list – flew out with screeching cries of annoyance at being disturbed.

They set off: Joel carrying his spear, Matata a *simi*, and Lucy her binoculars and bird book.

The glare off the pale sand made them screw up their eyes as they followed the broad expanse of the sand river upstream. Vervet monkeys peered at them from the trees along the edge making alarm calls at Fupi who was trotting beside Lucy. Grey and white go-away birds mocked them with their *gowarrr* calls. Iridescent bee-eaters swooped to catch dragonflies, and doves called from all around.

Lucy was becoming used to the wealth of wildlife everywhere but she still found it bewildering. She was trying to stay with the others but had to keep stopping to check out yet another new bird.

'Come on, Lucy,' called Kal.

'I've just seen a three-banded courser.'

'A what? I bet Mrs Sandford wears one of them.'

'What are you talking about?'

'Three-banded corset.'

'No, you idiot, a courser!'

'Whatever, but don't take all day.'

They came round a bend in the sand river. There was still no sign of water, but an enormous greyish brown bird – almost twice the size of the ground hornbills Lucy had previously seen – was poking about in some grass. It looked up as they appeared, and then stalked off.

Lucy was frantically juggling binoculars and book, before finally identifying it. 'It's a kori bustard.'

'Great,' said Kal, 'I've always wanted to see one.'

'It's Africa's heaviest flying bird,' said Lucy, reading from her book.

'It wasn't flying.'

'Oh, for goodness sake!'

Matata hissed and sniffed the air. He put his finger to his lips and hurried them out of the sand river.

'What is it?' whispered Lucy, when they had scrambled up the steep bank.

Matata said nothing, but beckoned and led them through the trees, continually looking around, testing the wind, and checking the ground. He led them past a clump of bushes. A pair of doves flew up with a clatter of wings and a ground squirrel scampered off. Then he pointed.

Lucy gasped and snatched up Fupi.

There in the sand river stood an enormous elephant – no more than thirty paces away.

'It's not Moshi?' she whispered.

'No,' said Joel. 'This one is a male. He is peaceful.'

And there, at last, was the water. The elephant had dug a hole in the sand with his tusks; it must have been more than a metre deep. He was dipping his trunk into the water at the bottom, sucking it up and squirting it into his mouth. Some impala were standing nearby waiting for their turn, but from the leisurely way the elephant was drinking, it would be quite a wait.

As they watched, some zebras and baboons came and joined the queue. But a young baboon which was feeling thirsty – or impatient – scampered to the water's edge and began to drink.

The elephant sucked up a trunk full of water, gave a deafening scream and squirted the baboon, which fled with terrified shrieks.

The children couldn't stop themselves from laughing. The elephant stared in their direction.

They froze.

The elephant seemed to frown; then flapped his great ears, and resumed its drink.

Lucy breathed out.

Joel signalled them to move back. 'That is where the water is, Lucy; under the sand. It is only a proper river in the rains – then it can be very dangerous to try and cross.'

'How did Matata know the elephant was there?' asked Kal.

Joel pointed to the ground. Footprints, like enormous dinner plates, led towards the river. 'You can see by the big footsteps that it is a male elephant.'

'You and Matata may be able to, but I can't,' said Lucy.

Joel smiled. 'And see, here.' He pointed with his spear at scuff-marks in the sand between the dinner plates. 'That is where his nose marks the sand.'

'His trunk,' said Lucy. 'Those marks are made by his trunk?'

Joel nodded. 'Can you smell that?' He lifted his head and sniffed.

Lucy sniffed. 'It's a sort of farmyard smell.'

'That's the elephant,' said Joel. 'The wind is blowing towards us, so we can smell him, but he can't smell us.'

'What would happen if the wind was blowing the other way?' asked Kal.

'That one would get angry.'

'And what would he—?' Lucy's words were cut short.

'*Ona!*' Matata was pointing to a distant hillside.

'What is it, Matata,' asked Ellie. 'What can you see?'

'I can't see anything,' said Lucy.

'It is Samson, returning,' said Joel. 'Look with your binoculars, Lucy.'

She put them to her eyes and searched the hillside. Eventually she located a minute dust plume moving down the hill. And Matata had seen that!

'Come. We will meet them.' Joel led them back to the Land Rover.

They sat in the shade and ate their picnic, and watched some baboons foraging under the trees on the opposite bank.

Lucy added a striped kingfisher to her bird list.

'What are those tracks that Fupi's sniffing?' asked Ellie, pointing to a trail that led across the dry sand towards the baboons.

Matata went and examined it. '*Simba*,' he called, '*dume*.'

Joel joined him; then beckoned the children down.

'It is a big male lion,' said Joel. 'See those feet.'

Lucy was glad the Land Rover was nearby.

'He has gone that way.' Joel pointed in the direction of the baboons on the far bank.

'Is he near?' asked Ellie.

'No, he crossed last night. He is now far. See, the baboons are not worried.'

Kal put his hand down and spread his fingers over one of the paw marks, but couldn't cover it. 'I wouldn't want to mess with him.'

'Someone's coming,' whispered Lucy. 'Look.'

They stared.

A man was pounding along the track towards them.

Chapter 23

An Angry Lion

The man saw them, waved and ran to join them.

'It's Reuben!' cried Kal.

'*Jambo*,' said Reuben, coming and shaking everyone's hand.

'Reuben,' said Lucy, 'what are you doing here?'

'Taking exercise.'

'Yes, but—'

'They're back!' cried Kal, as a Land Rover came into view.

Samson pulled up, and he, Craig and Dad climbed out and stretched.

The children hurried across. Lucy hugged Dad then rushed up to Craig, who had his arm in a sling. 'Welcome back.'

'Thanks, Lucy.' He was smiling and the tired look had left his eyes.

'How many bullets did they pull out?' asked Kal, grinning.

'About six. I lost count.'

Lucy's eyes widened. 'You are going to be all right?'

'Yeah, but the doc says I'll never play the violin again.'

'I didn't know you played the—'

'Lucy, it's a joke,' said Ellie.

Lucy blushed. 'Sorry.'

'You'll still be able to fly the plane?' said Kal.

'No sweat. So, how are you guys?'

'We've seen the most enormous elephant,' said Lucy. 'We were so close and—'

'Tell me as we drive back,' said Craig. 'I'll swap places with Joel.'

'Can I drive?' said Kal.

'Sure.'

***

What Kal found so fantastic about the dirt roads on the ranch was there were no pedestrians, no traffic and no speed limits.

128

The road surface reminded him of the running track where he trained every Tuesday night; they were a similar colour and had a—

A loud bang!

Lucy screamed.

The steering wheel was snatched from Kal's hands. He hit the brakes. His immediate thought was a shot.

The Land Rover veered off the track and stopped against a tree.

'What was that?' Kal looked wildly round.

'Blow-out,' said Craig.

'What?' Lucy was rubbing her forehead where it had banged on the windscreen.

'We've got a burst tyre,' said Craig. 'Now you know, Kal, why I make you keep your thumbs outside the steering wheel on these roads.'

Kal glanced at his hands. 'I guess that would have broken them.'

'Yup.' Craig climbed out of the vehicle followed by the others.

Samson pulled up in the other Land Rover, and he and Joel came to inspect the damage.

'Have you got a spare?' asked Lucy.

'Sure,' said Craig, 'but it'll take a while to change.'

Joel dragged out the high-lift jack from under the rear seat. Samson found the wheel-brace and began loosening the wheel-nuts.

'Can I help?' asked Reuben.

'No, we're good,' said Samson.

'Perhaps I'll carry on running, then. I need the training.'

'Rather you than me,' said Craig, grinning.

'Come on, Kal,' said Reuben, 'You can show me the way.'

'Me?'

'Why not? You're wearing shorts and trainers.'

'Yes, but—'

'*Tuende* – let's go then.'

Matata took off his flip-flops.

'Are you going to run as well?' cried Lucy. 'In bare feet?'

Matata grinned.

'I hope you two won't leave me behind,' said Reuben.

Kal turned and waved, and nearly tripped over a rock.

'We'll catch you up,' said Craig.

'No chance,' called Kal.

***

Kal couldn't believe it. He already had Reuben's autograph. But this! He was actually running with Reuben Kalima, with one of Tanzania's great athletes – one of the world's great athletes – a man who'd won an Olympic gold medal.

He kept glancing at Reuben, noticing the way he held his arms, how he kept his shoulders relaxed, and how his flowing stride was effortless. He tried to relax in the same way and copy that stride. His running became easier *and* he was going faster. This was it! This was how he'd got away from Rat-Man in the hills. His own running now seemed effortless. The three of them were eating up the ground.

The track led them through clumps of bushes. They came clear and Kal, who was leading, skidded to a halt.

Reuben and Matata nearly bumped into him.

A massive lion, its front paws on the body of a freshly-killed zebra, was in the middle of the track.

Kal stood transfixed and his eyes widened in terror.

The lion, a fully-grown male its muzzle covered in blood, stared unblinking at them swishing its tail slowly back and forth.

Kal felt his heart pounding. He tried to control his breathing, but it still sounded like a steam train. He hoped the lion couldn't hear it. His one urge was to run – but he knew that would be fatal.

'*Enda nyuma* – go back,' whispered Reuben. '*Pole, pole* – slowly.'

Kal didn't dare look behind. He was mesmerised by the lion's cold yellow eyes. His head began to swim.

The three of them edged slowly backwards, watching those unblinking eyes.

The lion climbed over the carcass and crouched down, still staring at them.

Where was Craig? Why weren't the Land Rovers coming?

The lashing of the tail increased. The lion started to creep towards them, never taking its eyes off their faces. The muscles in its shoulders rippled. Its great paws padded noiselessly on the ground. They *were* bigger than Kal's hand – much bigger.

Reuben gave a quiet hiss and they stopped.

The lion stopped. It crouched lower and laid its ears back. Then it started forward again. It made no sound: no growling, no roaring, no snarling. It just came slowly and silently towards them. Any moment, it would spring, and that would be it.

Kal found he was completely detached from what was happening. What he would feel?

He'd seen on TV, the way lions killed zebra and wildebeest. Did they kill people in the same way?

He was vaguely aware of a blur of movement.

The lion yelped as a rock hit its nose.

Matata picked up another. Ran at the lion with a great shout and threw the rock.

This was too much. The lion turned and fled with Matata in pursuit.

Reuben and Kal yelled, and Matata stopped. He hurled another rock.

Another yelp. The lion disappeared into some bushes.

Matata came loping back, a huge grin on his face.

'Matata, that was awesome,' said Kal.

They looked round at the sound of a vehicle. Craig drew up beside them. 'How's it going, guys?'

'I think I've done enough running,' said Kal.

***

They were now back at the house. Dad had gone off for a shower. Mum and Diana had finished fussing over Craig and had disappeared inside. Craig and Reuben were now in the office discussing ranch business, leaving the girls on the veranda listening to Kal's account of Matata's heroics.

'That guy was so cool,' said Kal. 'I don't know what would

have happened if…'

Fupi pricked her ears and gave a soft growl.

They looked round.

Two vehicles were approaching the house. One was a police car. The other was a Range Rover with broken headlights.

Chapter 24

Reuben Turns the Tables

Lucy watched fearfully as the vehicles drew up. 'Craig,' she called, 'I think you should come.'

'What is it?'

'Looks like trouble, big time,' said Kal.

Craig emerged from the office but Reuben stayed inside.

'What the…?'

Two policemen got out of the car.

Toad-Face and ole-Tisip – still wearing his T-shirt with the scary rat – got out of the Range Rover. They looked up briefly, then Toad-Face led the way onto the veranda.

'Good afternoon, Gideon,' said Craig, looking hard and cold.

Toad-Face ignored Craig's greeting but urged on one of the policemen.

He seemed very unhappy as he came forward. 'Mr Craig, I have a warrant for your arrest,' he said, holding up a piece of paper.

'Arrest! What for?' Craig didn't move.

'For abduction.'

'Abduction?'

The policeman indicated the paper. 'Abduction of a boy, Lengurai ole-Punyua.'

'Does he mean Matata?' whispered Lucy to Ellie.

Ellie nodded.

'What is all this, Gideon?' said Craig.

'You heard what the officer said.' Toad-Face urged the policeman forward.

He seemed even more unhappy.

'Mr Craig, I must ask you to come with us for further questioning in connection with this matter.'

'And, it would also be an opportunity,' said Toad-Face, in his silly voice, 'for you to tell the police why you have illegally taken over the Seki Hills, which belong to my friend ole-Tisip.'

'Gideon, that's Simba land and you know it,' snapped Craig.

'I think you will find the land registry document says something else.'

Craig said something rude.

Toad-Face ignored it. 'The boy will be coming back with us to his proper home.'

'No, he won't!' cried Kal.

'Yes, he will, my small friend.'

'And if we refuse?' said Craig.

'It is called obstructing the police in the course of their duty. The courts do not view such behaviour sympathetically.'

Craig's lips were tight. 'Kal,' he said, 'go and get Matata.'

'No!'

'Kal, just go. Trust me.'

Kal glanced fearfully round and ran off.

Reuben was still in the office.

Lucy didn't know whether or not he could hear what was going on, but she wished he'd come out. She didn't dare move to go and get him.

Mum and Diana appeared from inside the house, and looked in alarm when they saw the new arrivals and everyone looking worried.

'Lucy, what is it?' whispered Mum.

'Toad-Face and that other man want to take Matata away. They said something about him being abducted. And they want to arrest Craig.'

'What!'

'Ah, Mrs Bartlett, good afternoon,' said Toad-Face. 'I trust you have recovered from your little ordeal the other day.'

Mum glared at him.

Ole-Tisip looked venomous as he tapped his *rungu* against his leg. The rat on his T-shirt appeared even more menacing.

The policemen seemed extremely unhappy, but Lucy was relieved to see they made no move to clap Craig in irons, or whatever it was they did in Tanzania when they arrested people.

Kal and Matata returned.

When Matata saw what was happening, he made to run off but one of the policemen grabbed his arm.

'Let him go!' yelled Ellie.

'Enough of this nonsense,' snapped Toad-Face. 'We are taking this boy back to his home, and you, Craig, are under arrest for abduction and for further questioning.' He turned to the two policemen. '*Tuende* – let's go.'

'Just a moment, Mr Nagu.' Reuben emerged from the office.

The two policemen saw who it was, sprang to attention and saluted.

Reuben gave them a curt nod.

Lucy almost shouted for joy.

'Inspector Kalima, what are you doing here?' Toad-Face had a startled look on his face.

'Just visiting,' said Reuben. He held out his hand to the policeman who was holding the arrest warrant.

The man passed it over.

Reuben glanced at it, tore it up, and dropped the pieces on the floor.

'How dare you!' cried Toad-Face.

'You must excuse me, Mr Nagu,' said Reuben, 'but I couldn't help overhearing what you were saying.'

'So?' Toad-Face looked livid.

'I understand you are about to leave,' said Reuben. 'Before you do, there are a few points which perhaps need clearing up.'

'Such as?'

Reuben took out some papers from a folder tucked under his arm. 'James Msolla, Simba's solicitor, has had these drawn up. He asked me to bring them here.'

He offered the papers across but Toad-Face made no effort to take them.

Reuben sighed. 'Let me explain, then. These are court papers relating to one Lengurai ole-Punyua, known by the name of Matata. If you were to read them, you would see the boy is now legally adopted by Samson and Martha Mutugi of Simba Ranch in the district of Shinyanga.'

'Hurray!' cried Lucy. She wasn't sure what it all meant, except that Matata was safe.

Now it was Toad-Face's turn to look stunned, but the policemen were hugely relieved and the one who was holding Matata's arm let go.

Matata seemed bewildered, but Ellie hurried over to him and explained.

'Do you have anything you wish to say, Mr Nagu?' asked Reuben.

'This man and I are leaving.' Toad-Face turned and indicated Rat-Man should follow him.

Reuben nodded to the policemen and they barred the way.

'What is this?' cried Toad-Face.

'As I said, Mr Nagu, there are a few points which need clearing up,' repeated Reuben.

'Stop wasting my time, Kalima!'

'A moment, please. I believe Craig has something he would like to ask you.'

'What?'

'A number of things,' said Craig. His eyes were hard. 'Firstly, why did ole-Tisip and your men try to kill me?'

'Those were not my men.'

'They were!' cried Kal. 'I saw them in your Range—'

'They were employed by ole-Tisip to protect his property.' Toad-Face glared at Kal. 'I understand the one who shot you, Craig, was acting in self-defence.'

'That's monstrous!' cried Mum, 'Craig wasn't even holding his rifle when your man shot him.'

Toad-Face shrugged. 'I wasn't there. It's your word against his.'

'How dare you!'

Toad-Face ignored Mum's outrage and tried to barge past the policemen, but they blocked the way.

'Let me pass!'

'Mr Nagu,' said Reuben quietly, 'I believe you mentioned the Seki Hills.'

Toad-Face spun round and glared. 'They belong to ole-Tisip.'

'I don't think that is correct.'

'If you don't believe me, go and look at the land registry document.'

'I have,' said Reuben, 'and it shows the land known as the Seki Hills on the Simba Ranch is indeed registered in the name of Temes ole-Tisip and – I might add – Gideon Nagu.'

Toad-Face sneered at Craig. 'So, no more trespassing. And next time, my guards may not be quite so kind to you.'

Reuben raised his eyebrows, took a notebook out of his pocket and scribbled something. 'I thought you said the guards worked for ole-Tisip.'

'Don't try and be clever, Kalima!'

'Very well. Perhaps then, we could return to discussing the Seki Hills. The document to which you refer is a forgery.'

'Nonsense!'

Lucy noticed flecks of white spit forming in the corners of Toad-Face's letter-box mouth, and his eyes were all piggy as he tried to contain his anger.

'This is disgraceful! You produce a totally false accusation without a shred of evidence.'

'I have the evidence.'

Reuben looked quietly confident and Lucy could imagine him lining up for the start of the Olympic final. He probably had that same look then.

'I don't believe you.' Toad-Face tried to sound confident but uncertainty was creeping into his voice.

'Let me remind you, Mr Nagu, of a bit of local history.' Reuben went to the sideboard and poured himself a glass of water. 'As you know, I was posted for a while to the nearby police station at Shinyanga, and certain things happened during my time there which we couldn't explain.'

'I'm not interested.'

'Just hear me. One thing was the disappearance and probable murder of a respected Maasai elder: Punyua ole-Matunya, that boy's father.' He pointed to Matata, whose eyes were darting between Reuben and Toad-Face as he tried to follow what was being said.

'What are you accusing me of?'

'Nothing,' said Reuben mildly. 'I am merely telling you about some of the things which puzzled us. Another was: who was behind the persistent attempts to claim parts of Simba land?' He paused. 'Some of those questions are now beginning to make sense.'

'This is pure speculation, Kalima, and you know it.'

Reuben sighed. 'I will need to revisit the papers relating to the death of Matata's father—'

Toad-Face snorted.

'— and I may want to question certain people in the light of remarks I have heard today.'

Toad-Face glared. 'I warn you, Kalima, I have powerful friends and greatly resent your outrageous speculation.'

Reuben took a sip of water, but his eyes never left Toad-Face. 'Mr Nagu, as far as the ownership of the Seki Hills is concerned, there is very little speculation.'

'Precisely! They belong to ole-Tisip.'

'I don't think so,' said Reuben. 'You see, when Craig informed James Msolla and me, about a year ago, of a dispute relating to the Hills, the three of us went to the archivist in the Ministry of Land and Housing – who, incidentally, is a friend of Msolla's.'

'What's an archivist?' whispered Lucy to Ellie.

'Someone who looks after documents,' Ellie whispered back.

'Oh.'

'We explained the situation to him,' said Reuben, 'and he showed us the land registration document. There was no doubt then that the Seki Hills were included in the land belonging to Simba Holdings, the company in whose name the ranch is legally registered.'

Toad-Face started to say something, but Reuben held up his hand. 'A few months after our meeting, I received a call from the archivist telling me someone else had asked to consult the same document. In view of our concerns, he thought I might be interested to know. That person, Mr Nagu, was you.'

'So? Those are public documents. I have every right, as MP

for the area, to consult them'.

'Of course. But now, Mr Nagu, we get to the interesting part. A few weeks ago, the archivist informed me that you returned *again* to consult the document. Imagine his surprise when he discovered the original document had been removed and replaced with a forgery – and not a very good one – showing the Seki Hills registered in your name and that of ole-Tisip.'

'Don't you accuse me of forgery.' Toad-Face's eyes narrowed. 'I'm warning you.'

Reuben paused. 'Mr Nagu, perhaps I did not make myself clear. I apologise. What I said is not quite true.'

'Hah!'

'What I should have said was the archivist found the *copy* of the original document had been removed. He is a cautious man, and following your initial interest, he replaced the original document – the one which shows Simba Holdings as the rightful owners of the Seki Hills – with a copy. It was the copy which was removed. The archivist still holds the original.'

Toad-Face was like a deflated football. 'It's not true,' he whispered. But Lucy could tell he was beaten.

'Take them away,' said Reuben to the policemen.

'Your vehicle looks a bit the worse for wear,' called Craig, as Toad-Face and Rat-Man were led down the steps. 'Did you have an accident or something?'

Toad-Face's eyes narrowed. 'You haven't heard the last of this.'

'I think we have,' said Craig.

There were sighs of relief all round as the men left.

'Thank goodness you were here to sort that out for us, Reuben,' said Diana.

'I was really worried,' said Lucy.

'What will happen to—?'

Ellie's words were cut short by a crash and a shout which was followed almost immediately by a revving engine.

The next thing they saw was Toad-Face's Range Rover racing off at high speed.

Chapter 25

The Way of the Bush

They rushed to the edge of the veranda to see the windscreen of the police car smashed. One of the policemen was draped over the bonnet groaning. The other lay on the ground not moving.

'Quick!' yelled Craig. 'Kal, go and get Joel or Samson and bring one of the Landies.'

Kal raced off, with Matata following.

Reuben and Craig ran over to the policeman lying across the bonnet, who was beginning to recover.

'Lucy joined them. 'What happened?'

He says it was ole-Tisip with his *rungu*,' said Reuben.

'His club?'

'Yes, he hit both of them. They just weren't expecting it.'

'This guy's in a bad way,' said Craig, who was kneeling beside the other policeman. 'I think his skull's fractured. We need to get him to hospital as quickly as possible.'

Samson came running round the side of the house. 'What is it, Craig?'

'Ole-Tisip smashed this guy's skull with his *rungu*.'

Samson swore.

'Get your vehicle and take him to hospital. If they can't treat him in Shinyanga, tell them to call the Flying Doctor in Nairobi.'

'Right.' Samson ran off.

Ellie knelt beside the man, wiping blood away from his face. 'He's really bad. I hope Samson can get to the hospital in time.'

Joel came roaring round the side of the house in the open Land Rover, with Kal sitting beside him, and Matata clinging on in the back.

'We'll go after them,' shouted Craig. 'Reuben, you'd better come with us.'

'Right.' Reuben jumped in beside Matata.

Craig tore the sling off his shoulder, scrambled in beside Kal and slammed the door.

'Me too!' shouted Lucy. And before anyone realised, she squeezed in between Reuben and Matata.

Joel sped off.

'Lucy!' Mum's frantic cry was lost in the roar of the engine.

'You shouldn't have come,' shouted Craig.

'Too late.'

'Well, hang on.'

In the distance, they could see a plume of dust where Toad-Face's vehicle was speeding away.

'I reckon he's got about a three-minute start,' said Craig.

Joel knew the tracks and could drive fast. Soon they caught glimpses of the Range Rover through the clouds of dust being thrown up behind it. Gradually, the gap between the vehicles lessened, but Joel had to slow as they drove into the choking clouds which hung in the still air. They emerged from one of these to see ole-Tisip leaning out of his window shouting back at them and waving his *rungu*.

'We're gaining on them,' said Reuben. 'Well done, Joel.'

'He's gone the wrong way,' shouted Craig. 'That track leads to a swamp. He'll never get through there.'

The vehicle in front was slowing.

'See,' said Joel, 'no dust. The track is wet.'

'He's stopped,' cried Kal. 'He's trying to turn round.'

Joel slowed down and stopped.

They watched the Range Rover half turn, stop, go forward, stop. Then it tried to reverse. The engine was revving and mud was flying up from its wheels.

'He's stuck!' cried Kal.

'*Tembo*,' murmured Matata.

'What does that—?' Lucy gasped.

An elephant had stepped out from behind a thicket, and was standing no more than twenty paces from the Range Rover. It seemed puzzled by the vehicle and stood watching it. Without warning, it tucked its trunk down, flattened its ears and

141

charged. It hit the vehicle a shuddering blow.

The doors burst open.

Toad-Face leapt out of one side and Rat-Man the other.

'They're getting away!' yelled Lucy.

'Toad-Face isn't,' said Kal.

They watched in horror as Toad-Face tried to run off through the swamp, but he was stumbling and kept falling over.

The elephant ambled after him at an almost leisurely pace.

Toad-Face turned, a look of terror on his face as the elephant closed.

It reached out its trunk grasped him round the waist, and raised him high in the air.

Toad-Face screamed, his legs waved, and he hammered on the trunk with his fists, trying to break the crushing grip.

Lucy blocked her ears to shut out those terrible screams.

Then the screams abruptly ceased as Toad-Face was slammed into the ground.

It was Lucy's turn to scream.

The elephant picked up the limp body and slammed it down again. Then it placed a foot on the man's chest.

Lucy shut her eyes tight.

The silence was broken only by the call of a plover.

Craig was the first to speak. 'Where's Matata?'

Lucy's eyes flew open. 'He was here, beside me.' She looked wildly round.

'There!' shouted Kal, pointing. 'He's chasing Rat-Man.'

'That man killed his father,' said Joel.

'Where on earth did Matata find his bow and arrows?' muttered Craig. 'I thought I'd hidden them.'

Rat-Man turned and drew back his arm.

'Look out!' yelled Craig.

But Matata was too far away to hear the warning.

The *rungu* came whistling through the air.

Matata threw himself to the ground and rolled away just as it sailed past his head.

Now Rat-Man came at him with a drawn *simi*.

Those in the vehicle could do nothing except watch in dread.

'Matata, run!' yelled Kal.

Matata couldn't. He didn't have time to get up, or even notch an arrow into his bow. Rat-Man was upon him, slashing and stabbing with his *simi*. Matata rolled away again, and again, and a third time – each time, narrowly avoiding the razor-sharp blade as he tried to fend off the attack with one of his arrows.

Rat-Man grabbed the arrow and hurled it aside.

Matata was now defenceless. Once more, he twisted away.

Rat-Man hesitated.

Why?

Matata didn't wait to find out. He leapt to his feet and ran.

This time, Rat-Man didn't follow. He staggered and sank to his knees. He stared at his hands and screamed. The screams died in his throat and he slumped to the ground. His body twitched and then lay still.

The rat on his T-shirt no longer seemed menacing.

'What happened?' whispered Lucy.

'He cut his hand when he grabbed the arrow,' said Reuben.

'And the poison did the rest,' said Craig.

'Awesome,' breathed Kal.

'I guess the guy had it coming to him,' said Craig.

The plover was still calling.

'Look,' whispered Kal. 'What's Matata doing now?'

They watched, not daring to breathe.

Matata was walking towards the elephant.

'That is Moshi,' said Joel.

'What?' cried Lucy.

'This is where she stays. She has come back from the hills.'

Lucy hardly dared look. 'Matata will be killed,' she whispered, gripping the seat in front, her knuckles white.

'No,' said Craig. 'Watch.'

Matata was now standing in front of the elephant. His hands were held wide and he was talking to it.

Moshi seemed confused. She made no attempt to charge Matata but rocked on her feet making groaning noises. Then her legs buckled, she fell to the ground and rolled onto her side with a great sigh.

'*Kufa*,' murmured Joel.

'She's dead,' said Craig.

'Oh no!' Lucy put her head in her hands, and didn't raise it until a hand was placed on her shoulder.

'Come,' said Craig.

The others were gathered round the dead elephant. Matata was stroking its trunk and talking quietly to it.

'What's he saying?' whispered Lucy.

'He's telling its spirit it is now at peace.'

'Now what's he doing?'

Matata broke off a branch of green leaves from a bush and stuffed it into Moshi's mouth, murmuring to her as he did so.

'He is saying: sleep well, my friend,' said Craig. 'The Maasai have a special relationship with elephants and regard them almost like their own people. The green leaves are to send her on a peaceful journey.'

'That is so nice.' Lucy too whispered a message to Moshi. Then she sniffed and wiped a hand across her eyes.

'Come and see what Joel has found,' said Craig, leading her closer to the elephant.

Lucy was really nervous, but knew if she was going to be a wildlife vet, she would have to get used to such sights. Moshi had seemed huge that time she chased their Land Rover, but close up, she was enormous.

Joel scrambled onto her back and pointed to a mark behind the ear.

'What is it?' asked Lucy.

'It seems to be an old wound,' said Craig, 'but it's still very swollen.'

Joel took his *simi* from his belt and began cutting through the tough skin.

Again, Lucy knew she had to watch. She wasn't afraid of the sight of blood – and there was plenty of that – and it wasn't horrible, as she feared.

Craig and Matata scrambled up beside Joel, who was now digging into the wound.

'It goes very deep,' called Craig. 'I reckon it's some sort of abscess.'

'Would it explain her behaviour?'

'Could do.'

'*Aieeh*!' cried Joel. The whole of his arm was inside the wound. He withdrew it, holding something in his hand, which he passed to Craig.

Craig slid down off the elephant and showed Lucy and Kal.

'An arrowhead,' cried Kal.

'A poacher's arrow,' said Craig. 'The wood has rotted away but the arrowhead remained, working its way in towards her brain.'

'Poor Moshi,' said Lucy. 'That's awful.'

'Certainly explains why she was bad tempered.'

'How long has that thing been there?' asked Kal.

'Could be months or even years. There's no knowing.'

'And Moshi has been suffering all that time?' said Lucy.

'I guess when she bashed the Range Rover it dislodged the arrowhead or burst something in the brain, and that's what killed her.'

'I thought you said arrow poison could kill an elephant,' said Kal.

'It would if it was fresh. The poison on that arrow was probably old when the poacher fired it; that's why it didn't kill her at the time.'

'Not like Rat-Man,' said Kal.

'He wasn't quite so lucky.' Craig looked across at the body.

'You could call it the justice of the bush,' said Reuben.

'For him and Toad-Face,' said Kal.

'It's certainly saved the police and the courts some work,' said Reuben. 'But—' He glanced at Craig. '— I think you should find a better hiding place for those arrows.'

'Sure.' Craig nodded then checked his watch. 'We should get back.'

'Are you going to leave the bodies?' said Kal.

Reuben thought for a moment. 'There's no room to take them with us and it will soon be dark. Craig and I will come back first thing tomorrow.'

'But what about hyenas and things?' asked Lucy.

'Perhaps the justice of the bush will be completed by the undertakers of the bush.'

Craig nodded. 'It's the way of the bush.'

'And Moshi can go on her last journey in peace,' said Lucy.

Craig smiled. 'Time to go.'

Chapter 26

Dad Springs a Surprise

It was dark by the time they got back to find Mum, Dad, Ellie and Diana waiting anxiously for them.

'Lucy!' cried Mum. 'You should never have gone off like that. Whatever were you thinking of?'

But Lucy didn't want to talk. She felt so sad about poor Moshi. And seeing Toad-Face and ole-Tisip or Rat-Man – whatever his name was – that was really horrible, even if they got what they deserved.

'Craig,' scolded Diana, 'taking the children with you like that!'

'I didn't have much choice; things happened so fast.'

'Well, at least you're all back safely,' said Dad.

'We were so worried,' said Mum.

'We're okay,' said Kal.

'Yes, but there's no knowing what might have—'

'Are the policemen okay?' asked Craig.

'Samson and Onesmo have taken the injured one to Shinyanga,' said Diana, 'and Martha's looking after the other one. He was just bruised. But I still—'

'Mother, I think we all need a drink.'

'I'll get you some tea,' said Ellie.

'I think some of us might need something a bit stronger.' Craig's face relaxed into a smile.

***

The policeman, who had been hit in the stomach, was fully recovered by the next morning. So, immediately after an early breakfast, Craig and Reuben took him and Joel out to the swamp, but wouldn't let the children go.

Lucy was relieved because she didn't want to see poor Moshi again. She waved at the vehicle as they left then joined the others at the breakfast table.

Dad had just arrived. 'I hope you've recovered from all your

147

excitement yesterday,' he said.

Lucy shrugged. She still didn't want to talk about it.

'Your father has some news,' said Mum.

'Oh,' said Lucy in a flat voice.

'Don't you want to know how he got on at the university?'

'Whatever.'

'Some good news, Lucy,' said Dad. 'I'm pleased to say my assessment was correct. Professor Wafula, the head of the department of geology at Nairobi University, was in no doubt as to the quality of the material I took him.'

Lucy shot up in her seat. 'So everyone's going to be rich?'

'Lucy!' cried Mum.

'Well,' said Diana laughing, 'the government will claim a portion but it should be an end to our financial worries.'

'Simba is going to be all right, then?' said Kal.

'It certainly seems that way.'

'Isn't that splendid news?' said Mum.

'It's brilliant!' cried Lucy.

***

Craig, Reuben, Joel and the policeman returned around midday, towing Toad-Face's battered Range Rover which would be taken to the police station at Shinyanga.

The policeman confirmed it was obvious Mr Nagu and ole-Tisip – what was left of them – had been involved in an unfortunate accident with an elephant. These things happened in the bush. He would make sure the next of kin were informed.

'Look what we found in the back of the vehicle,' said Craig.

'My briefcase!' cried Dad.

'So Toad-Face did nick it?' said Kal. 'I told you he had a briefcase with him when he left the hotel.'

'He probably managed to distract you when you were registering for the conference, David,' said Craig.

'I'm so pleased to have it back,' said Dad. 'From now on I'll be more careful.'

'I wonder,' murmured Lucy.

An hour later, Samson and Onesmo returned and reported

148

the policeman with the damaged skull had been stabilised at the hospital in Shinyanga, and the Flying Doctor service would be taking him to Nairobi for an operation. His life was no longer in danger but he would be in hospital for a number of weeks.

'Poor man,' said Diana. 'I'm so pleased he's getting the best treatment.'

***

It was a late lunch for everyone that day.

'So much has happened in the last few days,' said Lucy, helping herself to salad, 'but there are still things I don't understand.'

'Such as?' said Craig.

'Did Rat-Man really kill Matata's dad?'

'Matata certainly thinks he did,' said Kal.

'I think he's right,' said Reuben. 'But all we know for sure is that Punyua – Matata's father – disappeared after some trouble at his *manyatta*.'

'What sort of trouble?'

'Ole-Tisip claimed Punyua's *manyatta* belonged to him and tried to throw him out. I was stationed at Shinyanga at the time and we were often being called in when there were fights. But ole-Tisip was backed by Nagu and there was nothing we could do. I was furious.'

'So what happened to Punyua?' asked Lucy, sitting down next to Reuben.

'He disappeared.'

'Murdered?'

'We think so,' said Reuben. 'And ole-Tisip was the main suspect. But the body was never found – probably dumped in the bush for the hyenas.'

Lucy shuddered. 'The undertakers of the bush.'

Reuben nodded. 'So no charges could be brought. Then ole-Tisip moved in and took over Punyua's *manyatta*.'

'The Maasai elders with whom we share the ranch were very angry but because ole-Tisip had Nagu's support, they couldn't do anything,' said Craig. 'Punyua was a good man. I knew him, but not well.'

'When Nagu, Toad-Face – whatever we call him – had ole-Tisip in place,' continued Reuben, 'he used him in laying claim to the Seki Hills.'

'But how did Toad-Face find out about the stones?' asked Ellie.

'From one of the Simba board meetings,' said Craig. 'We were discussing ways to solve our funding problems and I told the board I thought there were valuable minerals in the hills.'

'So when Toad-Face heard Dad was coming, he had to quickly forge the land registration document?' said Ellie.

'That's right,' said Reuben.

'And that's why he wanted Matata, to see if he could get more information from him,' said Kal.

'And when Toad-Face stole Dad's briefcase and found the maps with his notes on them,' said Ellie, 'he got the final details he needed.'

'Exactly,' said Reuben. 'We know he'd been interested in the ranch for a while. Now he knew the Seki Hills were the likely site for the minerals.'

'So he and Rat-Man put men in the hills to stop other people going there?' said Kal.

'Nagu was very crafty,' said Reuben. 'In everything he did, he made it look as though it was ole-Tisip – the one you call Rat-Man – who was organising things; whether it was getting Matata back, laying claim to the hills, or posting guards there.'

'But why did the guards shoot Craig?' asked Mum.

'That was probably a mistake.'

'Well, that's a relief, hey,' said Craig, rubbing his shoulder.

'Sorry, Craig,' said Reuben. 'I think one of the men panicked when they saw your rifle, but having shot you, they didn't then know what to do.'

'Was that why Rat-Man tried to catch me?' said Kal.

'He probably didn't want a witness escaping.'

'What would he have done if he'd caught Kal?' asked Lucy.

'Let's not think about it,' cried Mum.

'We won't know for sure what happened in the hills,' said Reuben, 'but I imagine ole-Tisip and Nagu had an arrangement to meet there.'

'I bet Toad-Face got a shock when Rat-Man and the other two men appeared with Mum, Dad and Craig,' said Kal.

'I guess he did, but he hid it pretty well,' said Craig. 'He gave those guys a right pasting and said we would be safe with him.'

'And we were foolish enough to believe him,' said Mum.

'By the time we realised he wasn't on our side,' said Craig, 'it was too late and we were imprisoned in ole-Tisip's *manyatta*.'

'But why did he take us to that dreadful place?' asked Mum.

'That I do know,' said Reuben. 'Nagu held you there while he went to Shinyanga to get the police and have Craig arrested on those charges he brought up yesterday, but when he got back with the police, you'd gone.'

'So he chased after us,' said Kal.

'Yes, with those two policemen. They thought they were going to be killed by the buffaloes. Nagu was yelling and screaming. The men were terrified and had to overpower him and drag him out of the driving seat.'

'But why did the police wait nearly a week before coming back?' asked Diana.

'It took that long before Nagu could get an arrest warrant.'

'So the first time,' said Craig, 'he didn't have a warrant?'

'No, and the police were very reluctant to go with him. But—' Reuben shrugged, '—Nagu could push people around.'

'No longer, thank goodness,' said Diana. She looked round the group. 'You know, I think we may need to find a new board member.'

***

Craig insisted on celebrating that evening. While he and Samson organised a fire under some massive acacia trees, Kal, Matata, Reuben and the other policeman – whose name was Elijah – carried down chairs and tables. Fancy a policeman being called Elijah, thought Lucy, as she, Ellie and Mum helped Diana and Martha get food ready.

Dad kept getting in the way and saying things like: 'you must give me something to do,' and then forgetting what it was. But no one minded.

Lucy remembered the barbecues the family sometimes had at home, when Dad pulled their rickety barbecue on wheels out from under the flowerpots in the garden shed, brushed off the cobwebs, and then couldn't get the charcoal to light because everything was damp.

The present setting was what barbecues ought to be like: a warm still night with a beautiful moon, a blazing log fire with its flickering light reflecting off the trees, a yummy smell of roast meat mixed with wood smoke drifting in the air, and the night sounds of Africa all around. She was only sorry Joel and the cattlemen weren't there because they ought to be sharing in the celebration – and there was a mountain of food.

'What's that noise?' said Mum.

A strange grunting sound was coming from beyond the trees – and it was getting nearer.

The fire flared, illuminating the edge of the clearing, and there with his spear and shield, was a Maasai warrior. He was stamping in time to the grunt, crashing his spear against his shield – and advancing towards them.

Fupi growled and Lucy quickly picked her up.

The fire flared again and Lucy saw other warriors following him. The hairs on the back of her neck prickled.

The grunting grew louder, and still the men advanced.

Suddenly, she realised: the warrior in the front was Joel! And the one behind was Onesmo, and then the other cattlemen – all in their traditional warrior dress, and all with spears and shields with intricate patterns painted on them. She stood up and cheered.

There was a call from Joel and the men gave a shout and stopped.

Everyone clapped.

The men laughed and came and shook everyone by the hand.

Craig and Reuben passed round drinks and the men settled down beside the fire, laughing and chatting.

Lucy thought it was a fantastic evening which only got better.

After everyone had eaten, Joel called out to the men and they formed a semi-circle, standing stiff as soldiers. Joel gave a command and they started bouncing. They kept quite straight and hardly bent their knees, but bounced higher and higher, grunting and nodding their heads in time to the bounce.

'Come on, guys,' called Craig, joining in. 'Sorry not the girls.'

But Lucy didn't take any notice. She found it really difficult bouncing without bending her knees. Everyone laughed but she didn't mind. Then Kal and Matata joined them – they were quite good, especially Matata. Craig stopped because his shoulder was hurting but Samson, Reuben and Elijah took his place, and the men cheered even louder. Dad said he wasn't going to make a fool of himself, but Lucy dragged him into the middle. He amazed everyone by being nearly as good as Onesmo. 'It's all that climbing up and down hills I do,' said Dad, embarrassed.

One of the men called out and everyone stopped. Reuben was pushed into the middle. The men started grunting again and this time Reuben had to bounce on his own. He winked at Kal and really started to bounce.

Everyone was grunting now and clapping. Even Fupi joined in, barking in time to the bounce. Lucy couldn't believe how high Reuben went – like he was on the moon.

Reuben grinned and stopped. He was hardly breathing.

'What's this?' cried Kal, picking up something from the ground. 'It fell out of your pocket, Reuben.'

'Oh no!' cried Reuben. 'I'm so sorry. Samson collected the post when he was in Shinyanga and asked me to pass this letter on.'

'Who's it for?' asked Lucy.

'It's addressed to Professor Bartlett.'

'Me?' said Dad. 'But I'm not a professor.' He took the letter from Reuben and opened it. 'Good Lord!'

'Who's it from?' asked Kal.

'It's a letter from the Dean of Science at the University of Nairobi.'

'Why's he written to you?'

'Well, I'm blowed.' Dad looked round the gathering,

beaming. 'He's offered me a temporary chair at the university while Professor Wafula goes on a period of study leave to the United States.'

'What do you want a chair for?' asked Lucy.

'Don't be silly, Lucy. It means Dad is going to be a professor,' said Ellie.

'A professor!'

'Hmm, Professor Bartlett,' said Dad. 'I rather like the sound of that.'

'That's fantastic, Dad,' cried Ellie. She and Lucy rushed up and hugged him.

'Cool, Dad,' said Kal.

'Will you accept?' asked Craig.

Dad thought for a moment. 'You know, I think I will. Professor Bartlett, eh?'

'Does that mean we have to come and live in Kenya?' said Ellie.

'Your mother and I will have to talk about it,' said Dad, 'but it's more likely she will stay with you while you are at school in England, and bring you out during the holidays.'

'You must come and stay at Simba,' said Craig.

'What, come out here for school holidays?' cried Ellie.

'Why not?'

'Craig, do you really mean that?' asked Mum.

'Of course. I insist.'

'That is mega awesome.' Kal shook his head in disbelief.

'Wow,' breathed Lucy. She picked up Fupi and hugged her.

ENDS

154

Watch out for further:

AFRICAN SAFARI ADVENTURES

The Elephant-Shrew
(Don't read this book if you're afraid of eagles.)

Lucy, Kal, Ellie, Matata, and of course Fupi, in helping to move a rare but dangerous antelope from the coast of Tanzania to Simba wildlife ranch, are thrown into further hair-raising adventures by the discovery of an ancient map, messages scratched on cave walls, and hidden ruins in the forest, all of which speak of a terrible bygone culture. But has that time really passed? Why does Matata find the ruins so scary? What happens in the under-water cave of the rock-cod? Who is the mysterious old man who never talks? And is the elephant-shrew quite what it seems?

"I have now read both of the books and I cannot wait until the third one comes out. I read the Elephant-Shrew in just one morning. Once I had started reading I just couldn't stop." (Amazon review, 1ˢᵗ edition).

The Buffalo-Weaver
(Don't read this book if you're afraid of hippos.)

Witchcraft comes to Simba wildlife ranch in Tanzania and Maasai cattle start dying. Very soon, Lucy, Kal, Ellie, Matata and Fupi the terrier become caught up in this nightmare which threatens even their lives as they face the terrors of raging rivers, evil omens, night-time chanting and devil buffaloes. Will the children be able to discover the source of the witchcraft? Even if they do, will they be able to destroy it, before it destroys the ranch – and them?

"This is the third volume and is as good as the first. Totally recommend this book! Warning, may cause uncontrollable desire to go to Africa." (Amazon review, 1ˢᵗ edition).

The Leopard-Tortoise
(Don't read this book if you're afraid of rhinos.)

Lucy, Kal and Ellie, with help from their Maasai friends Matata and Kiki, and support from Mrs Sandford the headmistress of their school in England, plan to set up a school for Maasai children on Simba Ranch. But poachers invade the ranch in search of rhinos and the plan seems doomed to fail. When Mrs Sandford comes to the ranch will she be the dragon they are used to? And will their combined efforts be sufficient to defeat the poachers, protect the rhinos and save the school?

In preparation: The Rhinoceros-Beetle

For Older Readers

COBRA STRIKE
(Sequel to African Safari Adventures but set some years later).

Terrorists are smuggling uranium ore out of Tanzania to build nuclear weapons. The top-secret security organisation Cobra recruits teenagers Lucy, Kal, Ellie, and their Maasai friends Matata and Kiki to infiltrate the operation. Where is the ore coming from? Where is it going? Who is masterminding the operation? To answer these questions Cobra operatives must survive the hazards of mountain jungles, the African bush and shark-infested caves. Then they face the sinister Chui and his accomplices...

Cobra Strike was shortlisted for the Wells Festival of Literature Children's Story Competition 2016.

ABOUT THE AUTHOR

Tony Irvin is a vet who went to Africa for 2 years and stayed for 20 where he became an expert on a disease of cattle and wildlife which no one outside Africa has ever heard of. He has camped among elephants, canoed among hippos, climbed Africa's highest mountain and photographed a rhino in his pyjamas. He now lives in wild Suffolk, UK, with his family and a mischievous Parson Russell terrier called Fupi. The nearest he gets to an off-road vehicle these days is a ride-on mower.

If you enjoyed this book, tell your friends and write a review for Amazon. And tell me: tonyirvin12@gmail.com

ACKNOWLEDGEMENTS

While living and working in East Africa, I spent many weeks on safari and nights camping in the bush. My grateful thanks to those knowledgeable people who shared that passion, and from whom I learned so much about Africa, its remote places, its people and its spectacular wildlife, in particular: Ken Bock, Simon Evans, Michael Gwynne, Lionel Hartley, Robin Newson, Peter Stevenson and their families; and to Bajila and Shillingi for showing me something of their bush craft. My grateful thanks to colleagues who read and commented on numerous drafts and rewrites, particularly: David Axton, Carolyn Belcher, Janet Bingham, Claire Frank, Ann Jessett, Wilf Jones, Sue Sawyer and George Wicker. Many thanks also to Catherine Duncumb and Cat Sawyer for artwork and to Nick Heard, who introduced me to flying light aircraft. Particular thanks to George Wicker for book production.

About the LITTLE FIVE

Everyone who visits East Africa hopes to see the **Big Five**: lion, elephant, buffalo, leopard and rhinoceros, but very few are aware of the **Little Five**, from which the AFRICAN SAFARI ADVENTURES take their titles.

If you are lucky enough to go on safari, watch out for:

The ANT-LION is an insect, the adult of which flies at night. It looks like a damselfly or small dragonfly. The immature stage (or larva) lives in the soil where it makes a small conical pit in which to trap ants. Look out for these pits under acacia trees in dry sandy soil.

The ELEPHANT-SHREW. Several species occur in East Africa, most of which are the size of large mice. One that occurs in coastal forests is the size of a small dog.

The BUFFALO-WEAVER is a black bird with a red beak, similar in size to a thrush. It nests in colonies, building an untidy nest of sticks.

The LEOPARD-TORTOISE occurs in dry bush and can be recognised by the black blotches on its sandy-coloured shell. (Unlike the animal from which it takes its name, it does not climb trees!).

The RHINOCEROS-BEETLE is one of the largest beetles in Africa. Only the male has the large "horn" from which this insect gets its name.

Amaze your friends by learning some simplified Swahili.

Hello	*Jambo*
How are you?	*Habari yako* (literally 'news your?')
Good or well	*Nzuri* (The answer to *Habari yako* is always *Nzuri* or *Nzuri sana*)
Very	*Sana* (Always comes after the word it qualifies e.g. *Nzuri sana*)
Bad	*Mbaya* (Similarly *Mbya sana*)
Thank you	*Asante* (Similarly *Asante sana*)
Goodbye	*Kwa heri* (literally 'to happiness.')
Okay	*Sawa*
Yes	*Ndiyo*
No	*Hapana*
Here	*Hapa*
There	*Huko*
Mister or sir	*Bwana*
Come	*Kuja*
Go	*Enda* (Let's go – *Tuende*)
Fierce or sharp	*Kali* (Fierce dog – *Mbwa kali*. Sharp knife – *Kisu kali*)
House	*Nyumba*
Water	*Maji* (Hot water – *maji moto*.)
Milk	*Maziwa* (Cold milk – *maziwa baridi*)
Tea	*Chai*
Machete	*Panga*
Car or vehicle	*Gari*

Some animals:

Lion	*Simba*
Elephant	*Ndovu* or *Tembo*
Buffalo	*Nyati* or *Mbogo*
Leopard	*Chui*
Rhinoceros	*Kifaru*
Hippopotamus	*Kiboko*
Giraffe	*Twiga*
Cat	*Paka*
Chicken	*Kuku*